MY FRIEND CHARLES

Francis Durbridge

WILLIAMS & WHITING

Cover design by Timo Schroeder

9781912582686

Williams & Whiting (Publishers)
15 Chestnut Grove, Hurstpierpoint,
West Sussex, BN6 9SS

Titles by Francis Durbridge published by Williams & Whiting

Murder At The Weekend – the rediscovered newspaper serials and short stories

Also published by Williams & Whiting:
Francis Durbridge : The Complete Guide
By Melvyn Barnes

INTRODUCTION

My Friend Charles was Francis Durbridge's fifth BBC television serial, transmitted in six thirty-minute episodes from 10 March to 14 April 1956. The producer/director, Alan Bromly, was to remain the guru for most of Durbridge's television serials, just as Martyn C. Webster had been for Durbridge's radio serials since the 1930s. The Durbridge/Bromly television partnership had made an excellent start with *Portrait of Alison* the previous year and maintained momentum with all the familiar Durbridge elements – numerous red herrings and cliff-hangers, together with the mantra "do not believe anything anyone says". All of this was expected by the numerous viewers who had been enthralled by Durbridge's earlier television serials *The Broken Horseshoe* (1952), *Operation Diplomat* (1952), *The Teckman Biography* (1953) and *Portrait of Alison* (1955).

By that time Francis Durbridge (1912-98) was firmly established as the pre-eminent exponent of the thriller serial on UK television, the master of plots that twisted and turned while his protagonist struggled in a murderous web spun by someone who remained concealed until the final episode. And the added factor was that his thrillers were supremely British, at a time when many television crime series came from the USA – a factor that applied also to his closest television rival, Nigel Kneale, whose science fiction serials featuring Professor Quatermass were similarly a huge draw.

BBC television repeated *My Friend Charles* from 3 June to 8 July 1956, described in the *Radio Times* as telerecordings, but sadly this never resulted in the serial's later release on DVDs. So although *My Friend Charles* was subsequently adapted as a cinema film and as a novel, only now can we fill that gap with Durbridge's recently discovered original television script.

But perhaps at this point it is appropriate to put Francis Durbridge in context for those who might not be aware of the full extent of his career, as by the time he turned to television he had already been the most popular writer of mystery thrillers for BBC radio since the 1930s. In 1938 he had found the niche in which he was to carve his name, when his radio serial *Send for Paul Temple* was a great success and his subsequent Paul Temple radio serials over several decades built an enormous UK and European fanbase. So it was natural that, while continuing to write for radio, he should join the rush of writers into the newer medium of television – and in 1952 *The Broken Horseshoe* became the first thriller serial on British screens.

After *My Friend Charles*, Durbridge's television serials – *The Other Man, A Time of Day, The Scarf* and many more – attracted an enormous audience internationally, just as his radio serials had done. Various countries produced their own versions, in their own languages and using their own actors, and Durbridge achieved iconic status when German commentators described his serials as *straßenfeger* (street sweepers) because so many people stayed at home to listen to them on the radio or watch them on television.

It is not surprising that *My Friend Charles* was quickly turned into a cinema film, because four film adaptations of Durbridge's Paul Temple radio serials had been made and had been followed by film versions of his BBC television serials *The Broken Horseshoe, Operation Diplomat, The Teckman Biography* (filmed as *The Teckman Mystery*) and *Portrait of Alison*. As always the producers of the film version of *My Friend Charles* did everything possible to ensure that their film would appeal to the widest cinema audience, with Durbridge himself being retained to write the screenplay under the new title *The Vicious Circle* (Romulus/Beaconsfield/Independent Film Distributors, 1957).

And very customary at that time, the principal television actors were supplanted by those who were a proven attraction for cinemagoers, with in this case the leading role of Dr Howard Latimer going to John Mills rather than television's Stephen Murray. Needless to say Mills did an excellent job as always, although we might assume (in the absence of a recording) that such a distinguished actor as Stephen Murray had already done so on television!

Yet there remains a mystery surrounding the cinema film *The Vicious Circle*, with falsehoods persisting on the Internet and in listings magazines that have long been disproved. Assertions that this film was based on a Durbridge television serial called *The Brass Candlestick* are totally incorrect, in spite of the fact that a brass candlestick as a murder weapon and as a criminal organisation's motif is central to the television serial *My Friend Charles* and the film follows the characters and plot of that serial. The film credits Durbridge while sadly failing to name his original television serial, but irrefutable evidence was provided by a report in the magazine *Variety* (30 January 1957) that "Last Monday Peter Rogers started filming a screen version of Francis Durbridge's thriller *My Friend Charles* with John Mills." Any remaining doubt was dispelled by the production notes on the 2008 DVD of the film, confirming that it was based on *My Friend Charles*. The film was released in the USA as *The Circle* and throughout Europe under various titles, but ironically it was released in some Spanish-speaking countries including Argentina as *El Candelabro de bronce*, which translates as *The Brass Candlestick*!

Somewhat later *My Friend Charles* was novelised (Hodder & Stoughton, September 1963), but uniquely for Durbridge it first appeared as a *Radio Times* serial in ten parts from 4 July to 5 September 1963. The novel's European translations appeared in Germany as *Charlie war mein*

Freund, in Italy as *...dai nemici mi guardo io* and in the Netherlands as *Mijn vriend Charles*.

Although one can speculate that *The Brass Candlestick* might possibly have been Durbridge's original working title for television, it is of course listed today among the most highly regarded Francis Durbridge television successes under its transmitted title *My Friend Charles* – so let's now enjoy his original television script.

Melvyn Barnes
Author of *Francis Durbridge: The Complete Guide* (Williams & Whiting, 2018)

This book reproduces Francis Durbridge's original script together with the list of characters and actors of the BBC programme on the dates mentioned, but the eventual broadcast might have edited Durbridge's script in respect of scenes, dialogue and character names.

MY FRIEND CHARLES

A serial in six episodes

BY FRANCIS DURBRIDGE

Broadcast on BBC Television
10 March – 14 April 1956
Produced and Directed by Alan Bromly

CAST:

Dr. Howard Latimer . . . . Stephen Murray
Nurse Kay . . . . Anne Ridler
Grace Frobisher . . . . Ena Moon
Geoffrey Windsor . . . . Bryan Coleman
Frieda Veldon . . . . Marianne Brauns
Laura James . . . . .Gillian Raine
Detective-Inspector Dane . . . . John Arnatt
Walt Armstrong . . . . Victor Brooks
Dr. George Kimber . . . . Geoffrey Chater
Ken Palmer .Francis Matthews
Robert Brady . . . . Rupert Davies
Charles Kaufmann . . . . .Marvin Kane
Joyce Edwards . . . . June Ellis
Waiter . . . . Bryan Kendrick
Veldon . . . . Anton Diffring
Det.-Sgt. Thomas . . . . Peter Wayn
Plain clothes policeman . . . . .Brian Moorehead
Plain clothes policeman . . . . .Alan Gore-Lewis

EPISODE ONE

OPEN TO: Harley Street, London. A busy morning in early Spring.

A taxi turns into the street passing a stationary ambulance, and finally coming to rest outside of one of the large houses. DR HOWARD LATIMER gets out of the taxi, pays the driver, and crosses towards the front door. He wears a dark overcoat, a homburg hat, and carries an attaché case. The camera tracks in tight on the brass plate on the door of the house which says "Dr Howard Latimer, M.D."

CUT TO: DR LATIMER's Consulting Room. A large, comfortable, extremely well-furnished room on the first floor of the house in Harley Street.

NURSE KAY is standing at the desk reading a copy of 'The Lancet', the well-known Medical Journal. She is rather an attractive woman in her late thirties. The door opens and DR LATIMER enters. He has disposed of his hat and coat and is now seen wearing a grey suit.

KAY: (*Turning*) Oh, hello, Doctor! I didn't expect you back until five o'clock.

LATIMER: The meeting finished at three. I called in at St Matthew's. Any messages?

KAY: Miss James telephoned.

LATIMER: Yes?

KAY: She asked me to remind you about this evening.

LATIMER: (*Crossing to his desk*) I hadn't forgotten.

KAY: Eight-thirty – the Savoy Grill.

LATIMER: Yes, I know. (*Indicates the magazine she is holding*) So you've seen The Lancet?

KAY: Yes, doctor. I've just been reading the article.

LATIMER: It seems to have caused quite a stir at the hospital. (*Looks down at the papers on his desk*) Well, Nurse?

3

KAY:	There's a Mrs Frobisher to see you, sir.
LATIMER:	(*Looking up*) Frobisher?
KAY:	Yes. She's a patient of Dr Kimber's. She wants to see you about her little girl.
LATIMER:	Oh, that's right. Is the child with her?
KAY:	Yes.
LATIMER:	All right. Send them up. (*He opens the Appointments Book on his desk*) Now, let me see, I've an appointment at six o'clock.
KAY:	Oh, I'm sorry, doctor. I forgot. That's been cancelled.
LATIMER:	Oh. (*He makes a note in the book; smiling*) Is there anything else you've forgotten, Nurse?
KAY:	No, I – (*A sudden thought*) Oh! A Mr Kaufmann telephoned.
LATIMER:	(*Surprised; putting down the book*) Kaufmann? Charles Kaufmann?
KAY:	Yes.
LATIMER:	When was that?
KAY:	About an hour ago. It was a trunk call, from Scotland.
LATIMER:	(*Amused*) Charles – Well, I'm damned!
KAY:	He said he'd ring back.
LATIMER:	I was only thinking of Charles in the bath this morning. The last I heard of him he was in Hollywood.
KAY:	(*Curious*) Hollywood?
LATIMER:	Yes, he's a film producer.
KAY:	(*Puzzled*) Is he a patient of yours?
LATIMER:	Good heavens, no! He's a friend. I suppose you'd call him my best friend. We were at Cambridge together.
KAY:	Whatever made him become a film producer?

4

LATIMER:	(*Laughing*) Well, he started by studying law, then he said he wanted to be a doctor, finally he changed his mind and went to Hollywood.
KAY:	I gather he's done very well for himself.
LATIMER:	(*Laughing*) Very. You leave that to Charles! (*Nodding*) All right, Nurse. I'll see Mrs Frobisher now.
KAY:	Yes, doctor.

KAY goes out. LATIMER turns towards his desk and picks up the copy of The Lancet; he looks at it for a moment and then puts it down and moves behind the desk. The door opens and NURSE KAY re-enters followed by GRACE FROBISHER who is a smartly dressed woman of about forty; she looks worried and a shade nervous.

KAY:	Mrs Frobisher, doctor.

LATIMER turns and crosses to shake hands.

LATIMER:	Good afternoon.
GRACE:	Good afternoon, doctor.
LATIMER:	(*Looking at KAY*) I thought your daughter was with you, Mrs Frobisher? I understood Nurse to say …
GRACE:	(*Interrupting him*) I'd like to have a word with you first, doctor. If I may?
LATIMER:	Yes, of course. (*Indicating the armchair in front of his desk*) Do sit down. (*She does. To KAY*) Show the young lady in when I ring.
KAY:	Yes, sir.

KAY goes out. LATIMER returns to his desk and sits facing GRACE.

LATIMER:	I understand you're a patient of Dr Kimber's?
GRACE:	Yes. He asked me to give you this note.

GRACE hands LATIMER an envelope.

LATIMER:	Thank you.

5

LATIMER opens the envelope, very quickly reads through the letter, then puts it down on his desk.

LATIMER: (*Pleasantly*) I've known Dr Kimber a very long time. We used to be neighbours.

GRACE: (*Nervously, a shade ill at ease*) Yes, so I understand.

LATIMER: (*Smiling*) Well, tell me about your daughter, Mrs Frobisher. What seems to be the trouble?

GRACE: (*Obviously worried*) She's not at all well. She hasn't really been well for the last three months. She can't sleep, she has the most dreadful headaches, and – she suffers from hallucinations.

LATIMER: (*Faintly surprised*) Hallucinations?

GRACE: Yes. Well, perhaps I should say, an hallucination.

LATIMER looks at GRACE for a moment, then he picks up the ruler off his desk.

LATIMER: (*Quietly, holding the ruler, looking at GRACE*) Suppose you tell me this story from the very beginning.

GRACE: Just over four months ago we moved to a house in Hampstead and Ann started a new prep school.

LATIMER: A day school?

GRACE: Yes. One afternoon – it was a Wednesday if I remember rightly – Ann left school rather earlier than usual. About a mile from the school there's a house called 'Heronswood', it's a large house standing in about twelve or thirteen acres. It belongs to a Colonel Hudson.

LATIMER: Go on, Mrs Frobisher.

6

GRACE: It was the beginning of October. The leaves were falling and there were lots of chestnuts. You know what children are like about chestnuts, doctor. When Ann reached the house she just couldn't resist it, she climbed over the fence. She stayed in the grounds of 'Heronswood' about a quarter of an hour and then took a short cut home through some rhododendron bushes.

LATIMER: (*Quietly; interested*) Go on.

GRACE: When she arrived home the poor child was in a dreadful state, I'll never forget it, doctor. It was some little time before she could even talk coherently. When she could talk, she told us an amazing story. She said she'd seen the body of a man in one of the bushes; she said there was blood all over his hands and face and he'd obviously been killed with a brass candlestick.

LATIMER: A brass candlestick?

GRACE: Yes. Apparently it was by the side of the body. She described the man, the candlestick, everything. Naturally my husband rang the police and within a matter of minutes they were searching the grounds. (*Shaking her head*) They found nothing. There was no sign of the man; no blood; no candlestick, nothing. They never did find anything.

LATIMER: Did the police question Colonel Hudson?

GRACE: Yes, of course. The Hudsons are extremely nice people, but they were confused and bewildered like everyone else. It's perfectly obvious it was either an hallucination or …

LATIMER: Or what?

7

GRACE: (*Lamely*) Or Ann just made the whole thing up.

LATIMER: (H*e studies the ruler for a moment*) Mrs Frobisher, tell me; before this incident happened would you have described your daughter as an imaginative child?

GRACE: No. Intelligent, yes – but not particularly imaginative.

LATIMER: Would you have said that she was temperamental in any way; highly strung?

GRACE: No, I don't think so.

LATIMER: You say she suffers from headaches?

GRACE: Yes, and she can't sleep, and she's terribly – well, it's difficult to describe it. Terribly – withdrawn.

LATIMER: When did you first take her to see Dr Kimber?

GRACE: In November.

LATIMER: Just after this happened?

GRACE: Yes.

LATIMER: This candlestick, Mrs Frobisher. The one your daughter saw, or thought she saw.

GRACE: Yes?

LATIMER: Have you ever seen one like it?

GRACE: (*A shade surprised by the question*) Why, yes. You can see them in most antique shops. You know the kind of thing: made of brass with a twisted stem.

LATIMER: You haven't actually got one like it – at home, I mean?

GRACE: No. I don't think we possess any candlesticks.

LATIMER: (*Changing the subject*) Mrs Frobisher, do you – or your husband – ever talk to your daughter about what happened that afternoon?

8

GRACE:	No. We did at the time, of course. We asked her a great many questions. But now, well, we just never refer to it.
LATIMER:	You refuse to discuss it, in fact?
GRACE:	Yes.
LATIMER:	Does she ever give you the impression that she'd like to discuss it?
GRACE:	We've made it quite clear that the whole incident must be completely forgotten.
LATIMER:	Was that Dr Kimber's advice?
GRACE:	It seems to have been everyone's advice.
LATIMER:	(*Smiling*) I see. (*He puts the ruler down*) Well, let's take a look at this little girl of yours, Mrs Frobisher.

LATIMER leans across the desk and presses a bell push. The camera tracks in tight on LATIMER's finger on the bell button.

CUT TO: The Consulting Room, later the same afternoon. *LATIMER is sitting at his desk writing a letter. He finishes it, blots it, and puts it in an envelope. He is addressing the envelope when the door opens and NURSE KAY enters. She has changed out of her uniform and is dressed for going home.*

LATIMER:	Are you just leaving, Nurse?
KAY:	Yes. Is there anything you want, doctor?
LATIMER:	No, I don't think so, thank you.
KAY:	Your friend hasn't telephoned again?
LATIMER:	(L*ooking up; his thoughts elsewhere*) Friend? Oh, Charles! No, I don't expect he will. He's probably on the way back to Hollywood by now. Goodnight, Nurse.

KAY: Goodnight, doctor. (*Turns, then hesitates*) Oh, you won't forget your appointment with Miss James.

LATIMER: (*Looking at her; a shade surprised that she should have reminded him of this appointment*) No, I shan't forget.

KAY: Eight-thirty.

LATIMER: Thank you, Nurse.

NURSE KAY smiles and goes out. LATIMER takes a cigarette from the box on his desk and lights it. He sits back in his chair. After a moment he takes a bunch of keys out of his pocket and unlocks one of the drawers in his desk. He takes out a leather bound book and places it on the blotter in front of him. As he picks up his fountain pen there is a knock on the door. LATIMER looks up, a shade surprised)

LATIMER: Come in!

The door opens and GEOFFREY WINDSOR enters. He is a neatly dressed, bespectacled man in his early thirties. He carries a copy of The Lancet.

WINDSOR: Dr Latimer?

LATIMER: Yes?

WINDSOR: I'm sorry to disturb you, sir – but could you spare me a few minutes?

LATIMER: Well – who are you exactly?

WINDSOR: Geoffrey Windsor, sir. (*Smiling*) Daily Courier.

LATIMER: (*Rising*) Daily Courier?

WINDSOR: Yes. (*Holding up the journal*) I read your article in The Lancet, doctor. I'd like to do a piece on it for the Courier.

LATIMER comes from behind the desk.

LATIMER: Look here, you can't come barging in like this! How did you get in here?

WINDSOR: I told your nurse I was from the electricity department. (*Smiling*) I had rather mixed feelings when she believed me. (*Politely; indicating the journal*) Is there any truth in this article, sir?

LATIMER: (*Bristling*) What do you mean – is there any truth in it?

WINDSOR: It's a simple question, doctor.

LATIMER: If you mean is Mysoterin a cure, the answer's no. Surely I've made that quite clear.

WINDSOR: (*Seriously*) Dr Latimer, my newspaper has two   million readers. If they were intelligent enough to read The Lancet as well as The Courier there isn't one of them that wouldn't be excited by your article.

LATIMER: You have my permission to reprint it.

WINDSOR: (*Smiling; shaking his head*) It wouldn't mean a thing. You know that as well as I do.

LATIMER: Then, what is it you want?

WINDSOR: More details. More information. How many people have been cured by this treatment?

LATIMER looks at WINDSOR for a moment and then picks up his copy of The Lancet. He opens the journal.

LATIMER: (*Reading*) 'It is not intended that this preparation be regarded as a cure and it does not replace, supplant, or exclude any other accepted method of treatment.' (*He puts the journal down on the desk*) I've nothing else to add, Mr Windsor. (*A curt nod*) Goodnight.

WINDSOR hesitates, then crosses towards the door.

WINDSOR: All right, doctor. I'm sorry to have disturbed you.

WINDSOR reaches the door, then changes his mind, turns, and moves back towards the desk.

11

WINDSOR: Dr Latimer, I've got to write something when I get back to the office. Would you mind giving me a few personal details – about yourself, I mean?

LATIMER: (*Faintly amused*) Young man, I'm a doctor – not a film star. What do I want with publicity?

WINDSOR: No, seriously, doctor. How old are you? Have you any hobbies? Are you married?

The telephone rings.

LATIMER: (*Curtly*) I'm thirty-six. I have no hobbies. I'm unmarried. Goodnight, Mr Windsor.

LATIMER ignores WINDSOR and picks up the telephone receiver. WINDSOR doesn't move. He stands watching him.

LATIMER: (*On telephone*) Hello? … Yes, this is Dr Latimer … (*Suddenly; delighted*) Charles! My dear fellow, how are you? … Where are you speaking from? … What on earth are you doing in Prestwick? … (*Laughing*) Well, let that be a lesson to you – more hurry less speed! … Oh, I'm all right, busy as usual … You sound more American than ever! … What … (*Seriously*) … Charles, that's going to be awfully difficult. I've got an appointment this evening … Well, can't someone else do this for you? … but, Charles, I don't know the girl and besides … What? … (*Faintly irritated*) Well, why can't she get a taxi or something? … Well, I'm pretty important, too! … (*Quickly*) All right! All right, old boy! If it's like that I'll do it! No, I'll ring you tomorrow at Claridges …Right … Goodbye, Charles! (*Replaces receiver*)

LATIMER looks at his watch; he is obviously irritated and a shade harassed. He looks up and notices that WINDSOR is watching him. A thought occurs to him.

LATIMER: Have you got a car handy?

WINDSOR: Yes. Why?

LATIMER: Would you like to do me a favour?

WINDSOR: What is it?

LATIMER: Run me to London Airport.

WINDSOR: (*Surprised*) What – now?

LATIMER: Yes – straight away.

WINDSOR: (*Hesitant*) Well –

LATIMER: (*Indicating the phone*) That was a friend of mine – Charles Kaufmann. He's a film producer. He's flown over from New York and they've landed at Prestwick because of engine trouble. He was supposed to meet a girl at London airport at half past seven. He's asked me to stand in for him.

WINDSOR: Who is this girl?

LATIMER: Some German film star or other. Why the hell she can't take a bus, I don't know.

WINDSOR: What's her name?

LATIMER: Oh, my God, now what was it? Frieda Vel …

WINDSOR: Frieda Veldon?

LATIMER: That's it! Have you heard of her?

WINDSOR: Of course I've heard of her! She's well-known in Germany. What's she coming over here for?

LATIMER: (*A shrug*) I imagine she's going to make a film. (*looks at his watch again*) He's asked me to pick her up and take her to Claridges.

WINDSOR: (*Suddenly*) Okay, I'm with you. Do you speak German?

LATIMER: No. Do you.

13

WINDSOR: Yes. (*Grinning*) You know, it's a jolly good job you didn't turf me out. I'm just what the doctor ordered.

LATIMER smiles.

CUT TO: A long shot of London Airport and then dissolve inside the main entrance of the airport, which leads, by escalator, to the Reception Lounge and Restaurant. Passengers, Porters, Uniformed officials etc pass to and from. *The camera tracks slowly up the escalator with a uniformed AIR HOSTESS. As the AIR HOSTESS steps off the escalator and walks away, the camera pans across to LATIMER, who can be seen standing near the entrance to the lounge. He is wearing his outdoor clothes and is obviously looking for someone. After a moment, he turns and the camera pans across to the balcony overlooking the escalator and the floor below. The main door opens and GEOFFREY WINDSOR enters. He sees LATIMER on the balcony and waves to him.*

CUT TO: *GEOFFREY WINDSOR is standing with his back to the main door. He is joined by LATIMER.*

LATIMER: Have you found her?
WINDOR: Yes, she was over on the other side. Come along, let's go back to the car!

CUT TO: *FRIEDA VELDON – an extremely attractive blonde – is sitting in the back of a car. She carries a handbag and a flat parcel which looks like a gramophone record. LATIMER enters the car and sits next to her.*

WINDSOR'S VOICE: (*Out of picture*) This is the gentleman I was telling you about, Miss Veldon – Dr Latimer.

FRIEDA: Es ist sehr nett von Ihnen nich zu treffen, Herr
            Dr Latimer, aber sie sollten sich wirklich die
            Muhe nicht gegeben haben.

WINDSOR takes his position in the driving seat.

WINDSOR: I'm afraid Dr Latimer doesn't speak German.

FRIEDA: (*She has a pleasant accent but speaks English
            with difficulty*) So? I'm sorry. I was saying,
            it's very kind of you to meet me, Dr Latimer.

LATIMER: Not at all. (*He takes a good look at Frieda;
            and likes what he sees*) Not at all. Have you
            got your luggage?

WINDSOR: Yes, it's in the boot.

LATIMER: (*Smiling*) So you're a friend of Charles?

*During the following dialogue, the car is driven from the
Airport.*

FRIEDA: Charles?

LATIMER: Charles Kaufmann.

FRIEDA: I hope we shall be friends. I do not know.

LATIMER: (*Amused*) You sound doubtful.

FRIEDA smiles, and gives a little shrug.

LATIMER: Charles was very sorry he couldn't meet you.
            Unfortunately, he doesn't arrive in London
            until tomorrow morning.

FRIEDA: Yes, your friend, Mr – ?

WINDSOR: Windsor.

FRIEDA: … Mr Windsor has explained.

*There is a pause. LATIMER takes out his cigarette case and
offers FRIEDA a cigarette; she shakes her head. LATIMER
looks at the case, and hesitates.*

LATIMER: Do you mind?

FRIEDA: No, of course not.

*LATIMER puts a cigarette in his mouth, returns the case to
his pocket and takes out a lighter. He flicks the lighter but it
doesn't work. He tries again, it still doesn't work. He looks at*

15

FRIEDA and smiles: flicks the lighter again, but it still refuses to light. FRIEDA is faintly amused; she takes a small book of tear-off matches out of her handbag and hands them to LATIMER. LATIMER grins, replaces his lighter and uses a match. He offers FRIEDA the book of matches and she shakes her head.

FRIEDA: You'd better keep them, it'll be cheaper than buying a new lighter.

LATIMER: (*Laughing*) Thank you very much.

LATIMER puts the book of matches into his waistcoat pocket.

LATIMER: Did you have a pleasant flight?

FRIEDA: Yes, it was very pleasant for … for … (*To WINDSOR*) Es war sehr angenehn fur diese Jahreszeit?

WINDSOR: Es war sehr angenehn fur diese Jahreszeit? (*To LATIMER*) For the time of year.

FRIEDA: (*Laughing*) It was very pleasant for the time of the year.

LATIMER: You speak very good English, Miss Veldon.

FRIEDA: I hope, perhaps … Is that right, I hope, perhaps …

LATIMER: Yes, that's right.

FRIEDA: I hope perhaps it will get better.

LATIMER: (*Without thinking*) Yes, I hope so, too. (*Quickly*) No, no, I didn't mean that! I meant …

FRIEDA: (*Amused*) We both hope so, Dr Latimer.

They smile at each other.

CUT TO: An ash-tray containing several cigarette ends.

The camera tracks back to reveal LAURA JAMES sitting alone at a small table in the lounge of the Savoy Grill. LAURA is about twenty-seven or eight and very attractive.

She has obviously been waiting for some little time and is extremely annoyed.

She looks at her wristlet watch, then rises, picks up her handbag and fur stole and crosses to the entrance to the lounge. As she reaches the door, LATIMER rushes in, breathless and embarrassed. LAURA immediately loses her expression of annoyance and covers her real feelings with a faintly artificial charm. LATIMER recognises the mood, but there is nothing he can do about it.

LATIMER: Laura, darling, I'm most terribly sorry I'm late!

LAURA: Late, Howard? An hour? What's an hour between friends?

LATIMER: Laura, I really am most frightfully sorry. I just couldn't help it, you see…

LAURA: Darling, there's nothing to worry about. It's not the first time. You've done it before.

LATIMER: Yes, I know, but this time it was –

LAURA: (*Before he finishes*) Different. It always is different, Howard. You were just leaving the hospital when the Matron said …

LATIMER: (*Irritated*) Look, sweetie, please, don't let's have a row about this!

LAURA: A row? We're not having a row, dear. Why should we? (*Sweetly*) Good night, Howard.

LATIMER: (*Taken aback*) What do you mean – good night?

LAURA: Good night, darling.

LATIMER: But aren't we going to have dinner?

LAURA: (*Apparently very surprised*) Haven't you had dinner, Howard?

LATIMER: Of course I haven't had dinner! What the devil do you think I've come here for?

17

LAURA: I thought you'd dropped in for a night-cap.
              (*She pecks his cheek with a kiss*) Good night,
              Howard. Ring me tomorrow – if it's not too
              much of an effort.
LATIMER: (*Trying to stop her*) Now don't be stupid,
              Laura! You can't just …
LAURA has gone. LATIMER stands staring after her;
annoyed and exasperated)

CUT TO: A taxi draws up to a Mews flat in Knightsbridge.
LATIMER gets out of the taxi, pays the driver and crosses to
the front door of the flat. He inserts his key and goes in.

CUT TO: Interior of LATIMER's flat.
A small hall leads to the main living room. Both the hall and
living room are tastefully furnished. The living room contains
a writing bureau; a table with drinks, telephone, small
radiogram etc. There is a large settee at right angles to the rest
of the furniture, which includes a newspaper and magazine
trough, television set, wing chair, etc. There is a walled
bookcase across a corner of the room which joins a large bay
window. Doors lead to the bedroom and kitchen. The entrance
from the hall is through an alcove.
Latimer enters the hall; he takes off his hat and coat and
throws them down. He still looks annoyed and depressed. He
enters the living room and crosses to the drinks table and
mixes himself a drink: after a moment he picks up the
telephone and is about to dial when he hesitates and changes
his mind)
LATIMER: To hell with her!
LATIMER replaces the receiver and takes his drink and
crosses the room to in front of the settee. Suddenly, he stops
dead, a look of complete astonishment on his face. The dead
body of FRIEDA VELDON is lying on the rug in front of the

settee. Her dress is torn and it is obvious that she has   been the victim of a violent assault. Her face, which bears witness to the attack, is turned towards the settee. Her handbag is by the side of the body. LATIMER rushes forward, kneels down, and turns the girl's face towards him. He is deeply shocked and horrified. He slowly rises, stares down at the body, then crosses to the table and picks up the telephone and dials. As he does so he stares down at the body, tense and bewildered.

CUT TO: *DETECTIVE INSPECTOR DANE is sitting in the wing chair in LATIMER's flat. LATIMER is sitting on the settee looking very worried. He has a whisky and soda in his hand. The body of FRIEDA VELDON has been removed. DETECTIVE INSPECTOR DANE is not the conventional detective; he is about fifty; well-educated; well dressed; a fastidious man. He is writing in a leather notebook with a silver pencil. After a moment, he looks up.*

DANE: I think I've got it all pretty clear now, doctor. Thank you very much.

LATIMER: I'm sorry I can't be more helpful.

DANE: On the contrary, you've been most helpful, sir.

LATIMER: (*Rising*)You see, what I don't understand is – how the devil did she get here?

DANE: (*Disarmingly*) We're not very far from Claridges, sir – she could very easily have walked.

LATIMER: No, I don't mean that, Inspector.

DANE: What did you mean, sir?

LATIMER: I mean, what the devil was she doing here, anyway?

DANE: Yes, well, of course, that's quite a different question, sir. (*Quite pleasantly*) She hadn't an appointment with you, doctor?

LATIMER: Of course she hadn't an appointment with me. I've told you, I never set eyes on her until this evening. In any case, I don't see patients here. I have rooms in Harley Street.

DANE: (*Smiling*) Yes, of course. Two hundred and thirty-nine …

LATIMER: (*Faintly surprised*) That's right.

DANE: You've probably forgotten but my wife came to see you about a year ago. Mrs Dane.

LATIMER: (*Remembering*) Oh, yes! Yes, of course.

DANE: (*Indicating his notebook; a shade apologetic*) Dr Latimer, do you mind if we run though this just once again? It is important.

LATIMER: Yes, of course.

DANE: (*Looking at his notebook*) A friend of yours, a film producer, called Charles Kaufmann, telephoned you this evening and asked you to meet a Miss Frieda Veldon at London Airport.

LATIMER: Yes. Charles was supposed to meet her but the New York plane was diverted to Scotland.

DANE: (*Nodding: still looking at the notebook*) You were driven to the Airport by a Mr Geoffrey Windsor, who is a journalist on the Daily Courier. You took Miss Veldon to Claridges and then you dashed off to the Savoy to keep an appointment with a Miss Laura James, your fiancée. (*Looks up*) Is that right?

LATIMER: Yes, but I didn't actually take Miss Veldon to Claridges. Mr Windsor did that.

DANE: (*Looking at his book*) You left them at –?

LATIMER: At Hyde Park Corner. I was terribly late for my appointment, so I jumped into a taxi.

DANE:	So you don't really know whether Mr Windsor took Miss Veldon to Claridges, or not?
LATIMER:	No, but, surely he must have done.
DANE:	Is Mr Windsor a friend of yours?
LATIMER:	No, he came to interview me about an article I'd written for The Lancet. He was in my room when Charles Kaufmann phoned, and he very kindly offered to run me to the Airport.
DANE:	I see. What time did you get to the Savoy?
LATIMER:	(*A shade irritated*) I've told you – half past nine.
DANE:	You were an hour late?
LATIMER:	Yes, my appointment was for eight thirty.
DANE:	But Miss James was still waiting?
LATIMER:	Yes, Miss James was still waiting.
DANE:	I see. (*Looks up; quite pleasantly*) There's nothing else, doctor? Nothing you've forgotten?
LATIMER:	No, I don't think so. There's nothing else I can think of.
DANE:	(*Nodding*) Mr Kaufmann arrives tomorrow morning?
LATIMER:	Yes, he's travelling overnight from Scotland. And by God, will I have something to say to him when I see him!
DANE:	Why? You think Mr Kaufmann might have had something to do with this?
LATIMER:	No, of course not, but if it hadn't been for Charles, I shouldn't be mixed up in it.
DANE:	Is he a very old friend of yours, sir?
LATIMER:	Yes, I suppose you'd call him a very old friend. We were at Cambridge together.

DANE:	Did Miss Veldon mention Mr Kaufmann at all?
LATIMER:	Yes; she said she hoped they'd get on well together.
DANE:	M'm. (*He looks at LATIMER for a moment*) She was rather an attractive girl, I imagine?
LATIMER:	You saw her, Inspector.
DANE:	Yes, but only after the murder – unfortunately. (*He looks at his notebook*) Was she well known in Germany?
LATIMER:	I understand so. I'd never heard of her.
DANE:	(*Looking up; smiling; closing his notebook*) Well, thank you very much, doctor. I expect we shall be in touch with you tomorrow when Mr Kaufmann arrives.

DANE stands and carefully fits the notebook and pencil into his waist coat pocket.

CUT TO: WALT ARMSTRONG, Features Editor of the Daily Courier, is sitting at his desk working on a new layout. The desk is a mass of newspapers, magazines, etc.

The telephone rings and WALT picks up the receiver.

WALT:	(*A slight North Country accent*) Hello? … I'm sorry, I didn't catch the name … Inspector Dane? … What can I do for you, Inspector? … Windsor? … Geoffrey Windsor? … There's no one here by the name of Windsor … Of course I'm sure! We've got a Geoffrey if he's any use to you … Bicklehurst. Sixteen. Spotty face. Can't make tea for toffee … sorry I can't help you. (*He replaces the receiver*)

CUT TO: *LAURA JAMES is sitting up in bed, surrounded by newspapers, pillows, etc. She wears a silk bed jacket. DETECTIVE INSPECTOR DANE is sitting by the side of the bed.*

DANE: (*With charm*) Miss James I do apologise for intruding like this. It's most kind of you to see me.

LAURA: What is it you want?

DANE: You've seen the newspapers and I imagine you've spoken to Dr Latimer, so there's no need for me to …

LAURA: No, no, I haven't. I haven't spoken to anyone. I've been so distressed.

DANE: Yes, of course.

LAURA: (*Indicating the newspapers*) Who is this girl, anyway? Frieda –

DANE: Frieda Veldon. She's a German film actress.

LAURA: Well, how on earth did Howard get mixed up with anyone like that? Is she a friend of his?

DANE: We don't know, Miss James, not yet. (*Pleasantly*) I understand you saw Dr Latimer last night, at the Savoy?

LAURA: Yes.

DANE: What time would that be?

LAURA: About half past nine.

DANE: What time did you arrange to meet?

LAURA: Eight thirty.

DANE: Why was Dr Latimer late, do you know?

LAURA: Oh, it was the usual story! He was detained at some hospital or other.

DANE: Is that what he told you?

LAURA: (*Faintly surprised*) Why, yes.

DANE: He didn't say anything about Miss Veldon, or London Airport?

23

LAURA: Why, of course he didn't! I'd never heard of
             this Veldon person until I saw the papers this
             morning.
DANE: I see. (*With a little smile*) Thank you, Miss
             James.
DANE rises.

CUT TO: DR LATIMER's Consulting Room, Harley Street.
*LATIMER is standing by the desk, on the telephone. He looks
tense and worried. He wears a different suit from the one he
wore the previous day.*
LATIMER: (*On phone*) … I'm still waiting! … Well,
             would you be kind enough to keep ringing the
             number? … Yes, of course there should be a
             reply … Yes, all right. Thank you. (*Replaces
             the receiver*)
*LATIMER sits at the desk and opens one of the drawers. The
door opens and DETECTIVE INSPECTOR DANE enters.*
DANE: Good morning, sir. May I come in?
LATIMER quickly rises from the desk.
LATIMER: Why, yes, of course. Inspector! (*Indicates the
             telephone on his desk*) I've been trying to get
             Claridges all morning. I haven't heard a word
             from Charles Kaufmann.
DANE: Mr Kaufmann's not staying at Claridges.
LATIMER: (*Surprised*) He's not?
DANE: No, sir.
LATIMER: Well, where is he staying?
DANE: (*A moment; looking at LATIMER*) At the
             Waldorf Astoria.
LATIMER: The Waldorf Astoria! That's in New York.
DANE: Yes, I know. (*He takes out his wallet and
             extracts a cablegram*)

LATIMER: Are you trying to tell me that Charles has flown back to New York?

DANE: According to our information he never left New York, sir.

LATIMER: But that's absurd! He spoke to me last night, on the telephone, from Scotland.

DANE: (*Shaking his head*) Not Mr Kaufmann. (*He looks at the cable and reads*) 'Charles Kaufmann arrived from Hollywood Monday. Still staying Waldorf Astoria'.

DANE hands LATIMER the cable. He stares at it in astonishment.

LATIMER: But this information is wrong! It must be wrong!

DANE: No, sir.

LATIMER: But I tell you Charles telephoned me from Scotland. I spoke to him. Geoffrey Windsor was here. He heard every word. I ... (*He stops and looks at DANE*) Have you seen Windsor?

DANE: No.

LATIMER: (*Angry*) Why not?

DANE: We're experiencing a little difficulty in finding him, sir.

LATIMER: Why, good God man, he's on the Daily Courier.

DANE: (*Shaking his head*) There's no one called Geoffrey Windsor on the Courier.

There is a tiny pause. LATIMER stares at DANE, obviously puzzled.

LATIMER: (*Quietly*) Are you sure?

DANE: I'm quite sure.

LATIMER: (*A sudden thought*) Well, perhaps I made a mistake. Perhaps it wasn't the Courier; perhaps it was some other newspaper.

DANE: We've checked all the newspapers.

LATIMER: (*A moment*) Inspector, I – don't like the sound of this.

DANE: (*Quietly*) I don't either, sir. You see no one, except yourself, appears to have seen this Mr Windsor.

LATIMER: The nurse saw him, she let him in. He told her he was from the electricity department …

DANE: That's what you told me last night, doctor – but apparently it isn't true. The nurse didn't see him.

LATIMER: How do you know she didn't?

DANE: I've asked her, sir.

LATIMER: What about Claridges? If Windsor took Miss Veldon …

DANE: (*Interrupting him*) I went round to Claridges last night, sir, immediately after I left you. They'd never heard of Miss Veldon.

LATIMER: Hadn't she a reservation?

DANE: No, sir. Neither had your friend Mr Kaufmann.

LATIMER looks at DANE for a moment and then slowly turns and crosses to the desk. He sits down, facing the INSPECTOR who sits on the arm of the armchair. DANE is not unpleasant in any way, his manner, if anything, is a shade sympathetic.

DANE: I saw Miss James this morning, doctor.

LATIMER: Well?

DANE: She confirms you were late turning up at the Savoy last night, but she says you didn't say anything about going out to the Airport. Miss James said you told her you'd been detained at the hospital.

LATIMER: That's not true.

DANE: That's what Miss James says, sir.

LATIMER: (*Tensely*) Well, she's imagining it! If you
               must know, Inspector, I had a row with her.
               She wouldn't let me get a word in edgeways.
DANE: (*Non-committal*) Oh, I see, sir.
LATIMER: (*Trying to control himself*) You don't believe
               me, do you?
DANE: (*Quietly*) I'd like to believe you, sir.
LATIMER: What does that mean?

A pause. DANE slowly takes a tiny diary out of his inside pocket.

DANE: You said last night that you'd never heard of
               Miss Veldon.
LATIMER: I hadn't until Charles Kaufmann phoned me.
DANE: This is Miss Veldon's diary. It was in her
               handbag.
LATIMER: Well?
DANE: (*Opening the diary*) According to this diary
               she had an appointment to see you this
               afternoon – at three thirty.
LATIMER: What!?
DANE: It's here, sir. (*Reads from the diary*) 'Dr
               Latimer, 239, Harley Street. Three thirty.'
LATIMER: I don't believe it!
DANE: It's in her diary, sir. (*A pause*) Have you got
               an appointments book?
LATIMER: Why, yes, of course.
DANE: May I see it?
LATIMER: (*Unhesitatingly*) Certainly.

LATIMER picks up his appointment book off the desk and hands it to DANE. DANE opens the book, turns over the pages; then suddenly looks up at LATIMER)

DANE: (*Surprised, and very puzzled*) Why, it's in
               your book as well, doctor. Three thirty. Miss
               Veldon.

LATIMER: But that's impossible!

LATIMER snatches the book from DANE and stares down at the open page. The telephone starts to ring.

DANE: Perhaps you forgot about the appointment, sir?

LATIMER: (*Tensely; still staring at the book*) Of course I didn't forget about it! Do you think I'm in the habit of forgetting my patients?

DANE: (*Quietly*) Well – it's in your book doctor.

The telephone continues to ring. LATIMER stands staring at the book; he is oblivious to the ringing of the phone. DANE moves to the desk.

DANE: (*Indicating the phone*) That may be for me, sir. I told my people they could get in touch with me here.

LATIMER doesn't reply, he is still staring at the book. The telephone continues ringing. DANE looks at LATIMER, hesitates, then picks up the receiver.

DANE: (*On the phone*) Hello? … Yes, Dane speaking … Oh, hello, Sergeant … (*seriously*) Where did you find it? … What's the car number? … I see … Well, he's here now, I'll ask him. (*He puts his hand over the mouthpiece and turns towards LATIMER*) Have you got a car, Dr Latimer – a Daimler?

LATIMER: Yes.

DANE: It's in Pelham's garage, Knightsbridge?

LATIMER: That's right.

DANE: What's the registration number?

LATIMER: VPE 132.

DANE looks at LATIMER and then slowly takes his hand off the mouthpiece.

DANE: (*On phone*) Yes, it's his car all right … (*a shade irritated*) No, there's no need for that. Get it down to the lab and tell them I want a

28

	report straightaway. (*He replaces the receiver*)
LATIMER:	(*Tensely*) What is it? What's happened?

DANE looks at LATIMER: he doesn't speak.

LATIMER:	(*Tense; rigid*) Inspector, you heard what I said – what's happened?
DANE:	(*Still looking at LATIMER: slowly*) The person who murdered Frieda Veldon used more than force, Dr Latimer.
LATIMER:	I know that. They used a weapon of some kind.
DANE:	Yes, sir.
LATIMER:	Well?
DANE:	(*Quietly*) We've found that weapon, sir.
LATIMER:	(*A moment; tensely*) Where?
DANE:	In your car, Dr Latimer. It was a brass candlestick.

LATIMER stares at the INSPECTOR in astonishment.

END OF EPISODE ONE

EPISODE TWO

OPEN TO: DR HOWARD LATIMER's Consulting
Room, Harley Street.

*DETECTIVE INSPECTOR DANE is standing by the
telephone looking towards LATIMER.*

LATIMER: (*Tense; rigid*) Inspector, you heard what I
             said – what's happened?

DANE: (*Still looking at LATIMER: slowly*) The
             person who murdered Frieda Veldon used
             more than force, Dr Latimer.

LATIMER: I know that. They used a weapon of some
             kind.

DANE: Yes, sir.

LATIMER: Well?

DANE: (*Quietly*) We've found that weapon, sir.

LATIMER: (*A moment; tensely*) Where?

DANE: In your car, Dr Latimer. It was a brass
             candlestick.

LATIMER stares at the INSPECTOR in astonishment.

LATIMER: A brass candlestick?

DANE: Yes, sir.

LATIMER: (*Shaking his head; bewildered*) But that's
             impossible!

DANE: Why is it impossible?

LATIMER doesn't answer; he stands deep in thought.

DANE: (*Quietly*) You haven't answered my question,
             doctor. Why is it impossible?

LATIMER: (*Looking up*) Yesterday afternoon a Mrs
             Frobisher came to see me. She told me that
             her little girl suffered from hallucinations and
             that four months ago, whilst searching for
             chestnuts in the grounds of a country house,
             the child saw – or thought she saw – the body
             of a man.

DANE: (*Watching LATIMER; curious*) Go on, sir.

33

LATIMER: According to Ann Frobisher the man was dead – murdered. The weapon was by the side of the body. It was a brass candlestick.

DANE stares at LATIMER; obviously puzzled.

DANE: Was this – 'hallucination' reported to anyone?

LATIMER: Yes, of course. The grounds were searched, but there was no sign of either the man or the candlestick.

DANE: I take it this story can be verified, sir?

LATIMER: Of course. Mrs Frobisher will verify it, or Dr Kimber.

DANE: Who's Dr Kimber?

LATIMER: He's the G.P. It was through Dr Kimber that Mrs Frobisher consulted me.

DANE: I see. (*He takes out his notebook*) Dr Latimer, you made a statement last night. Do you mind if we go through it again?

LATIMER: (*Faintly irritated*) Go ahead, Inspector, if it'll afford you any pleasure.

DANE frowns, is about to make a reply, then changes his mind and turns the pages of his notebook.

DANE: (*Looking at his notebook*) A friend of yours, a film producer called Charles Kaufmann, phoned you from Scotland and asked you to meet a Miss Frieda Veldon at London Airport. You were driven to the Airport by a Mr Geoffrey Windsor who, according to your statement, said he was a reporter on the Daily Courier. You left Mr Windsor with Miss Veldon in order to keep an appointment with your fiancée. Later, on returning to your flat, you discovered the body of Miss Veldon. Is that correct, sir?

LATIMER: Yes.

34

DANE:	You don't wish to alter the statement in any way?
LATIMER:	Why should I wish to alter it?
DANE:	Well, we've established that there isn't a Mr Windsor on the Courier. We've established that Mr Kaufmann didn't phone you from Scotland, and we've established that you did apparently have an appointment to see Miss Veldon.
LATIMER:	That's not true!
DANE:	It's in Miss Veldon's diary – and it's in your appointment book. (*He indicates the book on the desk*)

LATIMER presses the button on his desk for NURSE KAY.

LATIMER:	Nevertheless, I hadn't an appointment with her! I'd never heard of Frieda Veldon until Charles phoned me.
DANE:	(*Shaking his head*) Mr Kaufmann didn't telephone you, sir.
LATIMER:	Well, I think he did!
DANE:	He's in New York, doctor. If he'd telephoned you it would have been a trans-Atlantic call.
LATIMER:	(*Grimly*) The call was from Scotland.
DANE:	Then it wasn't Mr Kaufmann.
LATIMER:	(*A shade angry*) Look, Inspector, you've been asking me a lot of questions. Now I'd like to ask you one for a change.
DANE:	Go ahead, sir.
LATIMER:	Do you think I'm a liar?
DANE:	(*A faint smile*) That's a pretty pointed question, doctor.
LATIMER:	Don't be evasive, answer me. Do you think I'm a liar?

DANE: I think you've a very vivid imagination and – who knows? – perhaps a warped sense of chivalry.

LATIMER: What does that mean?

DANE: It's a polite way of asking whether you're covering up for anyone.

LATIMER: I'm not even 'covering up', as you call it, for myself. I've told you the truth. The whole truth. (*He shrugs*) If you don't believe me it's just too bad.

NURSE KAY enters.

DANE: It is indeed, sir.

LATIMER looks at the INSPECTOR, then takes the appointments book off the desk and turns towards the NURSE.

LATIMER: Nurse, did a Miss Veldon – a Miss Frieda Veldon – ever make an appointment to see me?

KAY: Not to my knowledge, doctor.

LATIMER: (*Opening the book*) You didn't write her name in my appointment book?

KAY: Why, no. I'd never heard of Miss Veldon until I read the papers this morning.

LATIMER nods and shows her the open book.

LATIMER: Whose handwriting is this – do you know?

The NURSE stares at the book in astonishment.

KAY: (*Shaking her head*) I've no idea.

LATIMER: (*Closing the book; dismissing her*) Thank you, Nurse.

The NURSE looks at the INSPECTOR and then goes out.

DANE: (*Holding out his hand*) May I take the book with me, sir?

LATIMER: (*Hesitant*) If you insist.

DANE: (*Smiling*) I'm not in a position to insist. If you don't wish me to take the book, just say so.

36

LATIMER: (*A moment; then*) There's no reason why you shouldn't take it.

LATIMER hands DANE the book.

DANE: (*Taking book*) Thank you. I'll let you have it back tomorrow morning. (*Casually, turning over the pages of the book*) If I should want to get in touch with you again, doctor …

LATIMER: (*Interrupting*) I shall be here until four o'clock, then I'm going to St Matthew's.

DANE: (*Still looking at the book*) Thank you, doctor.

LATIMER: (*A shade facetious*) Of course, if you're going to arrest me I should prefer that you did it here, rather than at the hospital.

DANE closes the book and looks up.

DANE: (*With the suggestion of a smile*) I'll bear that in mind, sir.

CUT TO: A tray on the desk in LATIMER's Consulting Room. The tray contains a glass of milk and several untouched sandwiches.

LATIMER is sitting at the desk smoking a cigarette. He looks tense and worried. NURSE KAY enters and crosses to the desk.

KAY: (*Indicating the tray*) Oh, doctor, this is too bad! You haven't eaten a thing – you haven't even touched the glass of milk!

LATIMER: (*Rising from the desk*) I'm sorry, Nurse.

KAY: Now come along, you must eat something.

LATIMER: (*Irritated*) For goodness sake stop treating me like a patient!

KAY: (*Unruffled*) If you act like a patient you must expect to be treated like one.

LATIMER looks at her, is about to say something, changes his mind and smiles.

LATIMER:	I see your point. I'm sorry, Nurse, I'm just not hungry.

NURSE takes the glass of milk and puts it on the desk, then picks up the tray.

KAY:	Well, I'll leave the glass of milk, anyway.
LATIMER:	(*Thoughtfully*) Nurse, what did you tell the Inspector when he asked you about the phone call – the first one, I mean?
KAY:	I told him it was a personal call for you from Scotland, from a Mr Kaufmann.
LATIMER:	And what did you say?
KAY:	(*Puzzled; she has been asked this before*) He asked me whether I spoke to Mr Kaufmann and I said no, only to the operator.
LATIMER:	(*Anxiously*) But you did tell him the call was from Charles Kaufmann?
KAY:	Yes, of course.

LATIMER nods. The NURSE looks at him, hesitates, then goes out. LATIMER returns to his desk and stubs out his cigarette. He stands deep in thought; perplexed and worried. Suddenly he reaches a decision, takes a diary out of his pocket and flicks the pages. He finds the information he wants, crosses to the telephone, and starts to dial. NURSE KAY enters.

KAY:	Dr Kimber would like to see you, doctor.

DR GEORGE KIMBER enters. He is a spruce, well-dressed man in his early fifties. At the moment he is a shade harassed. LATIMER replaces the telephone receiver.

LATIMER:	Why, hello, George! Come in!

KIMBER looks at the NURSE, waiting for her to leave before speaking. She goes out.

KIMBER:	(*Impetuously*) Howard, what on earth is going on? A man called Dane has been asking me the most ridiculous questions.

LATIMER:	Yes, I know. He's a police inspector.
KIMBER:	Well, what's this all about? Why is he interested in Mrs Frobisher?
LATIMER:	Haven't you seen the papers, George?
KIMBER:	No, I've been up North. I only got back this morning.
LATIMER:	A girl called Frieda Veldon was murdered – she was found in my flat.
KIMBER:	(*Quietly; shocked*) When was this?
LATIMER:	Last night.
KIMBER:	Well, what's this got to do with Mrs Frobisher?
LATIMER:	Apparently Miss Veldon was killed with a brass candlestick.

KIMBER looks at LATIMER; obviously bewildered.

KIMBER:	Look, Howard, I may be dense but I don't understand this. I sent Mrs Frobisher to see you because her daughter was ill.
LATIMER:	Yes, I know. But obviously in view of the coincidence I had to tell the police about it.
KIMBER:	What coincidence?
LATIMER:	(*Facing KIMBER*) Why, the fact that the girl was murdered with … (*A sudden thought*) George, you know all about Ann Frobisher – the candlestick – the man she saw – the hallucination …
KIMBER:	(*Staggered*) Hallucination?
LATIMER:	Yes. Four months ago she saw – or thought she saw – a dead man. There was a brass candlestick by the body.
KIMBER:	Who told you that?
LATIMER:	(*A shade annoyed*) Why, who do you think? Her mother, of course!

KIMBER: This is news to me, Howard. Mrs Frobisher simply told me her daughter suffered from insomnia and had very bad headaches. The child didn't respond to my treatment so I suggested a specialist. It was as simple as that.

LATIMER looks at KIMBER.

LATIMER: Is that what you told the Inspector?

KIMBER: What else could I tell him?

LATIMER: (*Softly; in despair*) Oh, my God …

KIMBER: (*Curious, yet a shade nervous*) Howard, this girl – the one they found in your flat – they don't think that you … (*Hesitates*)

LATIMER: (*Thoughtfully; worried*) I don't know what they think.

KIMBER: Was she a friend of yours?

LATIMER: (*Looking up*) No. No, I'd never heard of her until last night. (*Suddenly*) George, who is this Mrs Frobisher? What's her background? Where does she come from?

KIMBER: I met her at a cocktail party about six months ago. Her husband's an accountant. They live in Hampstead. They seem very nice people.

LATIMER: (*Tensely*) Then why did she lie to me? Why did she tell me this story?

KIMBER hesitates, looks at LATIMER; it is obvious he is a shade doubtful about him. The thought has also occurred to KIMBER that he must not get mixed up in anything remotely unpleasant.

KIMBER: I can't imagine why. (*Suddenly; looking at his watch*) Look, I'm due at the Middlesex at two-thirty. If there's anything I can do, give me a ring this evening.

LATIMER: (*Despondently*) All right, George.

KIMBER hesitates, then crosses to the door and leaves. LATIMER picks up the telephone receiver and dials. We hear the number ringing out and after a moment the receiver is lifted at the other end.

LATIMER: (*On phone*) Hello? Is that Primrose 1832?

CUT TO: *KEN PALMER holding the telephone receiver at the other end of the line; he is standing in front of an ornate cocktail cabinet. He is about thirty-two or three; good-looking, in a faintly impudent way. He is well dressed, smokes a cigar and holds a whisky and soda in his hand. He is in his living-room of an extremely modern flat in St John's Wood. There is a radiogram, a cocktail cabinet and a grand piano in a corner of the room, and numerous   photographs   of attractive girls.*

PALMER: (*Putting his drink down on the cabinet*) Hello? …

LATIMER: (*On the other end*) Is that Primrose 1832?

PALMER: (*In a disguised voice*) It is …

LATIMER: Could I speak to Mr Ken Palmer?

PALMER: (*Still disguising his voice*) Who wants him?

LATIMER: Dr Latimer …

PALMER: (*Pleasantly; surprised; his normal voice*) Why, hello, doc! I didn't recognise you! How are you, Squire?

LATIMER: I'm all right, Ken, but – (*Confidentially*) Are you alone?

PALMER: At two o'clock in the afternoon? My dear fellow, of course, I'm alone.

LATIMER: Look, Ken, I'm sorry to bother you, but – I'd like you to do me a favour.

PALMER: Any time, Doc – you know that. What is it?

LATIMER: Could you put me up for two or three days?

PALMER: Why, of course!

LATIMER:	It may not be necessary, but –
PALMER:	That's all right. Please yourself. I'll expect you when I see you.
LATIMER:	Thanks, Ken. Oh – er – don't mention this to anyone.
PALMER:	Why should I? (*A moment*) How's Laura?
LATIMER:	Oh, she's fine.
PALMER:	Good. Jolly good.
LATIMER:	(*Hesitant*) Well, I'll probably be seeing you.
PALMER:	I hope so, doc. Bye.

PALMER thoughtfully replaces the telephone receiver and picks up his drink. He crosses to the piano and, still obviously thinking of the phone call, leans against it. After a moment he takes a drink from the glass he is holding)

CUT TO: *LATIMER is sitting at his desk. He is drinking the glass of milk. He puts down the glass and opens a drawer. As he does so, NURSE KAY enters.*

KAY:	Inspector Dane would like to see you, doctor.
LATIMER:	(*After a moment*) Where is he, in the waiting room?
KAY:	No, he's in the hall. I didn't show him into the waiting room because …
LATIMER:	(*Interrupting her*) That's all right. Close the waiting room door and then show him straight up.

KAY looks at LATIMER, puzzled.

KAY:	Yes, sir.

She goes out. LATIMER takes a box of cigarettes out of the drawer and commences to fill his cigarette case from the box; when the case is full he closes the box. He leaves the box on the desk; closing the drawer. NURSE KAY shows in DETECTIVE INSPECTOR DANE. He looks serious, a shade worried. The NURSE goes out.

LATIMER: (*Looking up from his cigarette case*) Is this another consultation, Inspector?

DANE: (*Seriously*) I've seen Dr Kimber, sir.

LATIMER: (*Putting his cigarette case away*) So I understand.

LATIMER rises and comes from behind the desk.

DANE: There seems to be a slight difference of opinion.

LATIMER: Difference of opinion, Inspector?

DANE: About what Mrs Frobisher told you.

LATIMER: Have you seen Mrs Frobisher?

DANE: No, not yet.

LATIMER: Well, don't you think it would be a good idea if you did see her?

DANE: (*Interrupting him*) I think it would be a good idea if you came down to the station with me, sir.

(*A pause*)

LATIMER: Are you arresting me, Inspector?

DANE: I'm asking you to come down to the station with me, sir.

LATIMER: Why?

DANE: (*Hesitant*) I want you to make a statement.

LATIMER: But I've already made a statement!

DANE: Yes, I know, sir, but I think under the circumstances we'd better forget what you've told me so far.

LATIMER: (*Angry*) Why should we forget what I've told you? I've told you the truth!

DANE: Doctor, I'm only trying to help you. I wish you'd believe that.

LATIMER: You've made up your mind, haven't you? You think I murdered Frieda Veldon?

43

DANE: (*Patient*) No, sir, I haven't made up my mind, but I'd like you to come down to the station with me.

LATIMER: (*Bitterly*) You've got a job to do and you're going to do it, eh, Inspector? You're going to pin this one on me if it's the last thing…

DANE: (*Interrupting him; annoyed*) Dr Latimer, it's not my job to pin anything on anyone. Now, would you kindly do as I suggest?

LATIMER: (*After a moment*) What happens when we get to the station?

DANE: I shall ask you to make a statement in the presence of other police officers, and I shall warn you that anything you say will be taken down and may be used in evidence.

A pause. LATIMER looks at his watch.

LATIMER: I've a patient waiting to see me. May I go down and have a word with her?

DANE: Yes, certainly. You won't be too long, will you, sir?

LATIMER crosses the room towards the door.

LATIMER: I shall be about five minutes.

DANE: That's all right, I'll wait.

LATIMER hesitates.

LATIMER: I'm sorry if I was rude.

DANE: Just forget it, sir.

LATIMER: There are some cigarettes on the desk – help yourself.

LATIMER goes out. DANE crosses to the desk and takes a cigarette out of the box. He puts the cigarette in his mouth and extracts his lighter. As DANE flicks the lighter –

CUT TO: The exterior of the house in Harley Street.

After a little while LATIMER is seen rushing out of the house, dodging the traffic, and crossing the road. He half runs, half walks down the street, obviously in a desperate hurry but not wishing to attract too much attention to himself. A taxi swings round the corner and LATIMER immediately stops it. The taxi draws into the kerb; LATIMER gives hasty instructions to the driver and jumps inside.

CUT TO: *The taxi is drawing to a standstill, in a West End thoroughfare, near a public telephone box. LATIMER jumps out of the telephone booth and runs into the telephone booth. The cab remains by the kerb, waiting.*

CUT TO: *LATIMER in the telephone booth, dialling a number. He looks tense; anxious. We hear the ringing tone on the instrument. The ringing tone stops as the receiver is lifted at the other end. LATIMER presses button 'A'.*

CUT TO: *LAURA JAMES holding a cream telephone receiver.*

LAURA: Mayfair 1722 …

LATIMER: Laura, this is Howard …

LAURA: (*Annoyed*) How nice of you to phone, Howard! I wondered when you'd get round to it.

LATIMER: (*Tensely; quickly*) Laura, listen. I want you to do something for me. Bring your car round to my flat, straight away.

LAURA: Before you start issuing orders, Howard, don't you think you owe me an explanation?

LATIMER: (*Interrupting her; a shade desperate*) Look, Laura, I'm in a spot. I can't talk now. Do as I ask you, please, darling! Bring the car round straight away! (*He replaces the receiver*)

CUT TO: *LATIMER leaves the phone booth and runs back towards the waiting taxi. He jumps into the taxi, and as he slams the door the taxi drives away.*

CUT TO: LATIMER's flat.
LATIMER rushes out of the bedroom, carrying a dressing-gown; he puts the garment in a suitcase that also contains a sports jacket, flannel trousers, shirts, socks, ties, etc. He suddenly looks up. He has heard the noise of a car. He closes the case and crosses to the window.

CUT TO: A shot of the Mews, as seen through the window from LATIMER's eye level.
LAURA is getting out of a Sunbeam Talbot car which is parked in the Mews.

CUT TO: *LATIMER turns away from the window and crosses to the suitcase. The telephone rings. LATIMER stops dead, tense; he looks at the telephone on the table. He remains looking at the telephone, undecided whether to answer it or not. The telephone continues to ring. Suddenly LATIMER reaches a decision; he ignores the telephone, picks up his suitcase and goes out into the hall. The telephone continues ringing, then suddenly stops. In the hall, LATIMER puts down the suitcase and opens the front door. LAURA is in the doorway; she enters the hall.*

LATIMER: (*Taking LAURA by the arm*) Laura, my dear! Thank goodness you've come!
LAURA: Howard, what's this all about? Why do you want my car?

46

LATIMER:	I want to borrow it. I can't use my own because the police are watching it and ... (*Suddenly, holding out his hand*) Look, Laura, give me the key – please, darling, I haven't much time.
LAURA:	(*Holding the car key, looking down at the suitcase*) Where are you going?
LATIMER:	I'm going away for three or four days. I'll phone you later.
LAURA:	(*Interrupting him; tensely*) Howard, what really happened last night? Who was this girl that was murdered – was she a friend of yours?
LATIMER:	(*A shade desperate*) No, no, she was a friend of a friend of mine and ... Laura, give me the key, please!

LAURA looks at him, hesitates, then hands over the car key.

LATIMER:	The police think you murdered her, don't they?
LATIMER:	Yes.
LAURA:	Did you?
LATIMER:	No, of course I didn't!
LAURA:	Were you having an affair with her?
LATIMER:	(*Perturbed; taking hold of her*) No, there was nothing like that, I swear to you!
LAURA:	(*Facing him; puzzled*) Then why are you running away?
LATIMER:	(*Putting his hand on his forehead; tense and worried*) I've got to have time to think, Laura. Several things have happened during the past twenty-four hours. Not just the murder, several other things. Things I don't understand.

LAURA: You're making a mistake in running away,
            Howard. If you're innocent you've nothing to
            fear.

LATIMER: (*Shaking his head*) You don't realise what's
            happened, Laura. You just don't realise.
            Everything's against me at the moment.

LAURA: (*Quietly*) All right, Howard. You must do
            what you think is best.

*LATIMER is about to pick up the suitcase, then hesitates; he
is obviously very worried*)

LATIMER: Things haven't been too happy between us
            just recently, have they, Laura?

LAURA: (*Softly*) No.

LATIMER: (*Hesitant*) It's no good deceiving ourselves.
            It'll always be like this, you know. I shall
            keep you waiting in hotels, and bars, and
            trains – you'll keep losing your temper.

LAURA: (*After a moment*) I shall just have to get used
            to it, that's all.

*LATIMER takes her in his arms and kisses her, after a
moment he breaks away and picks up the suitcase.*

LATIMER: I'll phone you, darling. Now don't worry.

*He goes out. LAURA stands looking at the door, obviously
worried.*

CUT TO: *KEN PALMER is standing in front of the cocktail
cabinet in his flat, mixing a dry martini. He wears a dinner
jacket complete with button-hole. His overcoat is hanging
over the arm of a chair. LATIMER is sitting on the settee.*

PALMER: Now, for goodness sake, don't get me wrong,
            Squire. You can stay here as long as you like.
            But what's going to happen to that jolly old
            practice of yours if you hibernate for two or
            three days?

48

LATIMER: What's going to happen to the jolly old practice if they pin a murder charge on me?

PALMER: (*Smiling*) My dear old boy, I can see what's the matter with you! You've been reading too many thrillers, that's your trouble. The police don't pin murder charges on people, not in this country. (*He hands LATIMER the drink*) This is merry England, Squire!

LATIMER: Look, Ken – let's face the facts. You've heard my story. You've heard the whole thing right through.

PALMER: Well?

LATIMER: Do you believe me?

PALMER: Of course I believe you!

LATIMER: Would you believe me if we were complete strangers – if you were investigating the case?

PALMER: (*Hesitant*) Well –

LATIMER: Exactly! (*Rises from the settee*) I've been over this story not once, but fifty times. It's a fantastic story and I don't blame anyone for not believing it. But the point is, unless I can make people believe it I'm in a jam, and a pretty nasty jam at that.

PALMER: Well, I'm the simple type, Doc – you know that. I couldn't even get through medical school. But even I fail to see how doing a bunk is going to make anyone believe anything – except that you've done a bunk.

LATIMER: (*Faintly irritated*) I haven't done a bunk, as you so eloquently phrase it.

PALMER: (*Pleasantly*) But you have, Doc! The Inspector wanted you to go down to the station with him and you disappeared. If that isn't doing a bunk, what is?

49

LATIMER: Yes, well, I've got to have time to think, Ken.
             To sort things out. I can't sort them out while
             I'm trying to diagnose other people's
             troubles.

PALMER looks at LATIMER for a moment.

PALMER: You know, it seems to me that the key to the
             whole problem is this chap Windsor.

LATIMER: Yes, but the police don't believe he exists.

PALMER: (*Nodding*) Well, you've just got to prove that
             he does. Once you've done that they'll
             probably believe the rest of your story.

LATIMER: Yes, but how? How do I prove that Windsor
             exists?

PALMER: (*After a moment; nodding*) I see your point.

PALMER suddenly glances at his watch, then crosses to his overcoat.

PALMER: Look, Howard, I'm afraid I'll have to be
             going. I said I'd be there by eight o'clock.

LATIMER: Yes, all right, Ken.

LATIMER puts down his drink and helps PALMER on with his coat.

PALMER: I'm sorry about this ruddy party. I'd try to get
             out of it only …

LATIMER: Don't be silly, Ken. Why should you? Look,
             if I'm in the way at all, for Heaven's sake say
             so.

PALMER: (*Patting LATIMER's arm*) You're not in the
             way, Squire. I'm delighted to have you. It's
             just like old times. (*Straightens his collar*)
             Don't go to bed, old boy – unless you're
             particularly tired. We'll have another pow-
             wow when I get back.

LATIMER: Yes, all right, Ken.

PALMER: I gave you a key, didn't I?

LATIMER: Yes, but I shan't be going out.

PALMER indicates the cocktail cabinet and the box of cigarettes on the table.

PALMER: Well, you know where everything is. Help yourself.

LATIMER: Don't worry about me. (*Stopping him*) Oh, Ken …

PALMER: (*Turning*) Yes?

LATIMER: If you meet anyone we know …

PALMER: I shan't, old boy. It's not that sort of party.

LATIMER: (*Smiling*) Oh.

PALMER: (*Curious*) What were you going to say?

LATIMER: It doesn't matter.

PALMER: Go on.

LATIMER: I was only going to say, if you do meet anyone we know, I shouldn't mention my name in case … (*Hesitates*)

PALMER: Now, don't be silly, old boy! I'm not that stupid! (*Laughing*) See you later!

PALMER goes out. LATIMER looks at the drink he is holding, then suddenly finishes it and puts down the glass.

CUT TO: *A man's gloved hand pressing the bell push on the front door of KEN PALMER's flat. There is a tiny plate on the side wall, bearing the name: KEN PALMER. We hear the bell ringing out in the flat. The hand is removed. After a moment the door is opened by LATIMER. LATIMER faces ROBERT BRADY who is a rather heavily built man in his fifties; he carries a walking stick; a pair of gloves, and a grey homburg. He has a very slight Irish accent. His manner is strange but not by any means sinister.*

BRADY: (*Pleasantly*) Good evening! I trust I've got the right address. This is 23, Ivor Mansions?

51

LATIMER:	Yes, but I'm sorry Mr Palmer's out at the moment.
BRADY:	Oh. Oh, is that so? (*Smiling*) You're Dr Latimer?
LATIMER:	Er – yes.
BRADY:	I thought so.
LATIMER:	Have we met before, then?
BRADY:	No. No, we haven't, unfortunately. May I come in, doctor – just for a few minutes?
LATIMER:	Well, I'm afraid Mr Palmer won't be back until quite late …
BRADY:	(*Politely*) It's not Mr Palmer I came to see.
LATIMER:	(*Puzzled*) No?
BRADY:	(*Shaking his head*) No. (*Smiling*) It's you, Dr Latimer.

BRADY politely pushes the door with his walking stick and walks past LATIMER into the flat.

CUT TO: The main room of the flat.

BRADY enters, followed by a puzzled and faintly agitated LATIMER.

LATIMER:	Look here, what do you mean – you came to see me?

BRADY is taking off his gloves, slowly looking round the flat.

BRADY:	(*Ignoring LATIMER*) It's a simple statement, doctor. It shouldn't require an explanation.
LATIMER:	How did you know I was here?
BRADY:	(*Still looking about him*) Someone told me.
LATIMER:	Who?
BRADY:	It's not important.
LATIMER:	It is to me!

BRADY has finished his survey of the room and looks at LATIMER.

BRADY: There's a photograph of you in the evening
            paper. I don't know whether you've seen it or
            not. It doesn't do you justice.

LATIMER: Look here, what's your name? Who the devil
            are you?

BRADY: My name is Brady. Robert Brady. I'm a
            friend of yours.

LATIMER: You're no friend of mine!

BRADY: (*Quite seriously*) On the contrary: I'm a very
            good friend of yours, Dr Latimer.

(*A pause*)

LATIMER: Are you from Scotland Yard?

BRADY: Do I look as if I come from Scotland Yard?

LATIMER: (*Looking at BRADY; a moment*) No.

BRADY: I'm relieved to hear it. (*He looks round the
            room again*) You know, your friend has
            appalling taste. If you stay here any length of
            time I hope you'll make some changes.

LATIMER: (*Angry*) Never mind my friend! What is it you
            want? What are you doing here?

*BRADY looks at LATIMER for a moment, then apparently
makes up his mind*

BRADY: Last night you were driven to London airport
            by a man who called himself Geoffrey
            Windsor.

LATIMER: Well?

BRADY: The police don't think Mr Windsor exists –
            they think he's a figment of your imagination.

A moment.

LATIMER: (*Quietly; watching BRADY*) Well?

BRADY takes out his wallet from inside his coat.

BRADY: With my help you can prove that he does
            exist, Dr Latimer – that he is not a figment of
            your imagination.

53

LATIMER: What do you mean?

BRADY: (*Opening his wallet*) I have a photograph of
              you – a much nicer photograph than the one
              in the newspaper.

LATIMER: (*Puzzled*) A photograph of me?

BRADY: Yes. It was taken last night at the airport.

LATIMER: (*Tensely*) When?

BRADY: (*Smiling*) Just as you were getting into Mr
              Windsor's car. Would you care to see it?

BRADY holds up the photograph so that LATIMER can see it.
It shows LATIMER and GEOFFREY WINDSOR standing by
WINDSOR's car at the entrance to the Airport.

LATIMER: (*Tensely*) Why did you take that photograph?

BRADY: I had a shrewd suspicion it might be of value.

BRADY returns the photograph to his wallet; puts the wallet
in his pocket.

LATIMER: Are you trying to blackmail me, Mr Brady?

BRADY: (*Apparently interested*) Is that a possibility?
              Are you a wealthy man, doctor?

LATIMER: No.

BRADY: Then why should I wish to blackmail you?

BRADY crosses to the armchair and sits down; he looks up at
LATIMER.

BRADY: You know, I'm disappointed in you. I thought
              a man in your position would inevitably be a
              good judge of character. You're not. In an
              incredibly short   space   of   time   you've
              mistaken me for both a   detective   and   a
              blackmailer. It should be patently obvious
              that I'm neither.

LATIMER: Then what are you?

BRADY: (*Smiling*) I've told you. I'm a friend of yours.

LATIMER: If you're a friend of mine you'll give me the
              photograph. (*He holds out his hand*)

54

BRADY: (*Apparently sincere*) I've every intention of
                giving it to you – eventually.
LATIMER: (*A moment; quietly*) What is it you want?
*LATIMER sits on the arm of a chair; takes a cigarette from
the box on the table.*
BRADY: (*Quietly; serious*) I want you to answer some
                questions, Dr Latimer. They're really quite
                simple.
LATIMER: (*Taking out his cigarette lighter*) Well?
BRADY: Last night – at the airport – did Miss Veldon
                give Mr Windsor anything?
LATIMER: (*Puzzled*) Give him anything?
BRADY: Yes. A letter – an envelope – a parcel – a
                packet – anything?
LATIMER: No, of course she didn't.
BRADY: You're sure?
LATIMER: Well, she certainly didn't while I was there.
                She may have done afterwards, of course.
LATIMER flicks his lighter; it doesn't work.
BRADY: What was Miss Veldon wearing?
LATIMER: (*Surprised*) What was she wearing?
BRADY: Yes.
LATIMER: A brown suit with fur on it and a little red hat.
BRADY: And her shoes?
LATIMER: Her shoes?
BRADY: Yes. Did you notice her shoes?
LATIMER: Good heavens, of course I didn't. Why should
                I?
*BRADY nods, satisfied. LATIMER looks at him, tries his
lighter again, but it doesn't work.*
BRADY: What happened to Miss Veldon's luggage?
LATIMER: It was put in the boot of the car.
BRADY: By whom?
LATIMER: By Geoffrey Windsor.

BRADY: So you never actually saw it?
LATIMER: (*Thoughtfully*) No, I didn't.
BRADY: Was Miss Veldon carrying anything?
LATIMER: Yes, a handbag and a brown paper parcel.
BRADY: Have you any idea what was in the parcel?
LATIMER: (*After a moment*) It looked like a gramophone record.
BRADY: (*Pleased*) I see.
LATIMER: (*Bluntly*) Now, do I get the photograph?
BRADY: (*Apparently quite pleased with LATIMER*) Yes, you get the photograph, Dr Latimer.

BRADY puts his hand in his pocket for the wallet, then hesitates.

BRADY: Oh, there's just one other question.
LATIMER: Well?
BRADY: (*Smiling*) She didn't give you anything, by any chance?
LATIMER: (*With almost derision*) Of course she didn't! Why on earth should she? I'd never seen her before.

BRADY nods and takes out his wallet. LATIMER flicks his lighter again; it still doesn't work. He examines the lighter and a sudden thought occurs to him. BRADY is extracting the photograph from the wallet.

LATIMER: (*Without thinking*) Wait a minute …
BRADY: (*Looking up*) Yes?
LATIMER: (*Faintly amused*) As a matter of fact she did give me something: she gave me a book of matches.
BRADY: When was that?
LATIMER: While we were in the car. (*Shows BRADY his lighter*) This thing wouldn't work.

BRADY looks at LATIMER with almost a new interest.

BRADY:	(*Quietly; casual*) Have you still got the matches?
LATIMER:	Yes, I think so. They're in my other suit, at the flat.

BRADY closes his wallet.

BRADY:	Get me the matches, Dr Latimer, and I'll give you the photograph.
LATIMER:	Are you serious?
BRADY:	Perfectly serious.
LATIMER:	(*Annoyed*) But I can't get them! I've told you, they're at my flat.
BRADY:	I'm in no hurry. I can wait. (*Looks at his watch*) It shouldn't take you long at this time of night.
LATIMER:	(*Irritated*) But you don't understand, I don't want to go back to the flat! If I do that, the police are bound to …
BRADY:	(*With a shrug; about to rise*) Very well. It's entirely up to you, Dr Latimer.
LATIMER:	(*Stopping him*) No, wait! If I get you the matches, you'll give me the photograph?
BRADY:	I've already said so.

BRADY sinks back into the chair. LATIMER looks at him for a moment and then crosses to the telephone. He picks up the receiver and starts to dial. BRADY sits watching him)

BRADY:	Who are you phoning?
LATIMER:	My fiancée.

LATIMER turns towards the phone.

CUT TO: *LAURA's car, with LATIMER at the wheel, is parked in a side street in Knightsbridge. LAURA walks towards the car from the far end of the street. As LAURA arrives at the car, LATIMER immediately opens the door and jumps out.*

LAURA:	It's all clear. There's no one there.
LATIMER:	Are you sure?
LAURA:	Yes, I've been round the block twice.
LATIMER:	(*Kissing her on the cheek*) Thank you, darling. I'll ring you later.

CUT TO: The living room of LATIMER's flat.

LATIMER quickly enters from the hall, switches on the main light, and crosses to the bedroom. As LATIMER enters the bedroom the telephone starts to ring. LATIMER comes out of the bedroom and stands in the doorway; he is looking down at the book of matches in his hand. LATIMER moves slowly into the room, apparently oblivious to the ringing of the telephone. Suddenly, he looks up, realises that the telephone is ringing and crosses to the table. He puts his hand on the instrument and then instinctively hesitates; after a moment he lifts the receiver.

LATIMER:	(*On phone*) Hello?
MAN's voice:	(*On the other end*) Is that you, Howard?
LATIMER:	Who is this?
MAN's voice:	(*Impatiently; yet in a good humour*) Who the devil do you think it is? It's Charles!
LATIMER:	(*Astonished*) Charles!
MAN's voice:	Yes, Charles, old boy. Charles Kaufmann. Look, Howard, I've been trying to get in touch with you all day …
LATIMER:	(*Tensely; interrupting him*) Charles, where are you? Where are you speaking from?

Before LATIMER completes his sentence a shadow falls across his face, there is a thud, and the receiver falls from his hand. LATIMER falls forward, crashing on to the table, and finally on to the floor, the telephone receiver dangling over the side of the table. GEOFFREY WINDSOR is standing over LATIMER, a revolver in his gloved hand. It is obvious that he has hit LATIMER with the butt of the revolver. WINDSOR wears a soft hat, a smart tailored overcoat, and seems completely unperturbed. He picks up the receiver and replaces it in the cradle, cutting off the call. He stares down at LATIMER for a moment and then stoops and picks up the book of matches. He stares at them. They look like an ordinary book of tear-off matches. The words "DER KERZENHALTER" are printed on the cover.

CUT TO: The Living Room of LATIMER's flat; about fifteen minutes later.
The telephone is ringing. LATIMER is still on the floor, although he is gradually regaining consciousness. He eventually manages to rise but has to hold on to the table for support. He shields his eyes; stands rigid, still holding the table. After a moment he straightens himself, rubs the back of his neck, then looks down at the telephone which is still ringing. He stretches out to lift the receiver and at that precise moment the telephone stops ringing. With a tense, quick movement LATIMER snatches up the receiver.
LATIMER: Hello? Hello? … Damn! Hello? …
The dialling tone can be heard on the receiver. LATIMER slowly replaces the phone.

CUT TO: The front door of KEN PALMER's flat.
After a moment, LATIMER arrives; he looks tired, dejected, and distinctly worried. He feels in his inside pocket and produces the door key. As he inserts the key in the lock he suddenly looks up, obviously surprised. From inside the flat can be heard the sound of a piano being played. LATIMER hesitates, then unlocks the door and enters the flat.
CUT TO: Inside the flat.
KEN PALMER – seen from LATIMER's eye level – is sitting at the piano. He looks up, nods to LATIMER, and continues

playing. LATIMER looks around the room. DETECTIVE INSPECTOR DANE is sitting in the armchair, smoking a cigar, a glass of whisky in his hand. There is a suggestion of a smile on his face.

END OF EPISODE TWO

EPISODE THREE

OPEN TO: Inside KEN PALMER's flat.

KEN is sitting at the piano. LATIMER is looking at DETECTIVE INSPECTOR DANE who is sitting in the armchair. He has a drink in his hand.

PALMER: I'm afraid you've got a visitor, Doc.

DANE stands.

LATIMER: (*Looking at DANE: not too friendly*) So I see.

DANE: Good evening, Dr Latimer.

LATIMER: Good evening. (*To PALMER; surprised*) Where's Brady?

PALMER: (*Puzzled*) Brady? Who's Brady?

LATIMER: A Mr Brady called to see me just after you left. He asked me to – (*hesitates*) get something for him.

PALMER: (*Shaking his head*) I haven't seen him.

LATIMER: How long have you been back?

PALMER: About half an hour. I found the Inspector on the doorstep.

LATIMER: But wasn't Brady in the flat?

PALMER: (*With a little laugh*) No, of course not, there was no one in the flat. Who is this fellow Brady?

DANE: Is he a friend of yours?

LATIMER: No, I'd never seen him before.

PALMER: Well, how did he know that you were staying here?

LATIMER: I don't know. (*A note of sarcasm*) How did you know I was here, Inspector?

DANE: (*Unperturbed*) It's our business to know these things, sir.

LATIMER: Well, perhaps it's Mr Brady's business, too. (*To PALMER*) I'm sorry to put you to all this trouble, Ken.

PALMER: No trouble at all, Doc.

63

LATIMER:	(*To DANE*) It won't take me two minutes to pack, then I'm ready. (*Moves across to bedroom*)
DANE:	(*Politely*) Ready for what, sir?
LATIMER:	Aren't you going to arrest me?

DANE sits back in the armchair and picks up his drink again.

DANE:	Who said anything about arresting you?
LATIMER:	You did.
DANE:	When?
LATIMER:	This afternoon.
DANE:	I asked you to come down to the station and make a statement. I didn't say I was going to arrest you.
LATIMER:	(*Irritated*) Well, doesn't it amount to the same thing?
DANE:	You did a very stupid thing this afternoon, Dr Latimer. It's a good job you've got me to deal with, sir.
LATIMER:	Why you, in particular?
DANE:	(*Drinks; then puts down his glass*) I have a reputation for being a little unorthodox. An undeserved reputation, I assure you, so don't try and take advantage of it.
LATIMER:	If you haven't come here to arrest me, what the devil have you come for?
PALMER:	(*To LATIMER*) Howard, I don't want to chip in on this – but I think you've got hold of the wrong end of the stick.
LATIMER:	What do you mean?
PALMER:	I think the Inspector's on your side. He's trying to help you. He's not trying to trick you into anything.
DANE:	(*To PALMER*) Thank you, sir.

LATIMER:	Look, Ken, the Inspector doesn't believe a word I say, so …
DANE:	(*Interrupting him*) Doctor, that's not true.
LATIMER:	(*Turning to DANE tersely*) Do you believe what I told you about Geoffrey Windsor – about going to the Airport – about meeting Miss Veldon?
DANE:	(*Pleasantly*) Yes.
LATIMER:	You do?
DANE:	Yes, sir.
LATIMER:	(*Almost an accusation*) Something's happened! Something's made you change your mind!
DANE:	(*Shaking his head*) Nothing's made me change my mind. I've made certain investigations. The outcome of those investigations have substantiated – in parts – the story you told me about Geoffrey Windsor.
LATIMER:	You mean, someone saw me at the Airport?
DANE:	(*With the suggestion of a smile*) Yes.
LATIMER:	Who?
DANE:	One of the nurses from the Mayfair Clinic. She was meeting a friend of hers from Paris. She saw you and a young man – presumably Windsor – getting into a car. Her description of Windsor tallied with the one you gave us.
LATIMER:	Thank God for the Mayfair Clinic!
DANE:	(*Smiling*) I've also interviewed the taxi-driver.
LATIMER:	Taxi-driver?
DANE:	The one that took you to the Savoy; you picked him up at Hyde Park Corner.
LATIMER:	(*Remembering*) Oh, yes – that's right!

DANE: He saw you get out of a car and say good-bye to Miss Veldon. He also gave us a description of Windsor.

LATIMER: (*Relieved; and faintly pleased with himself*) So my fantastic story wasn't quite so fantastic after all, Inspector.

DANE: (*Quietly*) There are still one or two curious features, Dr Latimer.

LATIMER: Such as?

DANE: Well, Miss Veldon was found in your flat – and her name was in your appointment book.

LATIMER: (*Dogmatic*) Miss Veldon hadn't an appointment to see me, and I didn't put her name in my book.

DANE: I know you didn't, because it's not your handwriting, but someone did.

PALMER: (*To LATIMER*) Could it have been this chap Windsor?

DANE: (*To LATIMER*) Was he ever left alone in your consulting room?

LATIMER: (*Thoughtfully*) No. Wait a minute. I left him outside the room when I went out to get my coat and hat. That was when we were leaving for the Airport.

DANE: M'm. (*He takes out his notebook and opens it*) I saw Mrs Frobisher this afternoon. She confirms what Dr Kimber told me.

LATIMER: She does?

DANE: Yes. She says she consulted you because her daughter was suffering from insomnia and bad headaches. She completely denies your story about the hallucination, the dead man, the candlestick.

PALMER: What do you mean – she denies it?

66

DANE: She denies ever having mentioned a dead man, or a candlestick, to Dr Latimer.

LATIMER: But that's nonsense! Why should I make up a story like that if it wasn't true?

DANE: I'm not suggesting that you did make it up, doctor. I'm simply telling you what Mrs Frobisher told me. (*Glances at his notebook*) And there's still the phone call of course. The one that started the whole business. (*Looks up at LATIMER*) We know, for a fact, that Charles Kaufmann didn't make that call. He's in New York.

LATIMER: (*Irritated*) Charles isn't in New York! He phoned me again tonight, just over an hour ago.

DANE: (*Interested*) Kaufmann did?

LATIMER: Yes. Look, I'd better tell you what happened. (*To PALMER*) After Ken left, the man I told you about – Brady – called to see me. He produced a photograph of Geoffrey Windsor. He offered to give me the photograph in return for some matches.

PALMER: (*Incredulously*) Matches?

LATIMER: Yes. Brady asked me if Miss Veldon had ever given me anything, and I suddenly remembered a book of matches she gave me when my lighter wouldn't work. I went back to the flat to get them; they were in the suit I wore last night.

PALMER: Why did Brady want the matches?

LATIMER: I don't know, but he seemed to think they were important.

DANE: (*Nodding*) Go on …

LATIMER: While I was in the flat the phone rang. It was
                Charles Kaufmann.
PALMER: (*Interested*) What did he say?
LATIMER: He said he'd been trying to get in touch with
                me. I asked him where he was staying and he
                was just about to tell me when – wham! –
                someone hit me on the back of the head.
                When I came round I was on the floor: the
                matches had disappeared.
DANE: Who was it that hit you?
LATIMER: I don't know, I never saw him. He must have
                been in the flat when I got there.
DANE glances at PALMER.
PALMER: Did you have a chance to examine the
                matches?
LATIMER: Yes, it was just an ordinary book of matches
                with a name – an advertisement – I imagine –
                on the cover.
DANE: What was the name?
LATIMER: Oh, it was in German. (*Hesitant; uncertain of
                his pronunciation*) Der Korzen –
DANE: (*Correctly*) Der Kerzenhalter?
                K.E.R.Z.E.N.H.A.L.T.E.R.?
LATIMER: Yes, that's it.
PALMER looks at DANE.
PALMER: Do you speak German, Inspector?
DANE: (*Casually*) Yes, a little bit. Der Kerzenhalter
                … (*He looks at LATIMER*) It means – The
                Candlestick.

CUT TO: LATIMER's flat.
LAURA puts a tray on the table.
LAURA: (*Calling*) It's ready, Howard!

LATIMER: (*From bedroom*) Yes, all right, Laura! I'll be
              out in a minute.

LAURA puts her jacket on, then sits and pours coffee.
LATIMER enters.

LATIMER: M'm – smells delicious.

LAURA: I wish you'd let me get you some bacon and
              eggs, Howard.

LATIMER sits beside LAURA.

LATIMER: I couldn't face them, darling, not at this hour
              of the morning. What time's your train?

LAURA: Half past nine.

LATIMER: You haven't got a lot of time.

LAURA: (*Drinking her coffee*) I'll be all right.

LATIMER: Is this aunt of yours expecting you?

LAURA: (*Laughing*) She's been expecting me for the
              last three months. (*Drinking her coffee*) What
              are you doing today, Howard?

LATIMER: (*Also drinking his coffee*) I'm at St Matthew's
              most of the day.

LAURA: That's in Curzon Street.

LATIMER: Yes, that's right.

LAURA: I wonder if you could do something for me?

LATIMER: What is it?

LAURA: I ought to have picked up a pair of shoes
              yesterday from a shop in Baker Street.

LATIMER: I'll pick them up for you if you like.

LAURA: I wish you would. I've got the address here
              somewhere.

LATIMER: I'll see you back here about half past eight.
              Then we'll go and have some dinner.

LAURA: Yes, all right. (*Looks at him*) And Howard …

LATIMER: (*Looking up*) Yes, darling?

LAURA: Try not to worry.

LATIMER:	I'm not so worried as I was, not nearly so worried, but I'm still puzzled, Laura. There's so many things I don't understand.
LAURA:	Yes, I know. (*After a moment*) This morning when you phoned and asked me to come round, I suddenly realised something. Although you consider Charles your best friend, you've really seen very little of him in the past two or three years. I've never even met him.
LATIMER:	I saw him about a year ago; we had lunch together.
LAURA:	Yes, but people change, Howard.
LATIMER:	What do you mean? What are you getting at, darling?
LAURA:	This business started with a phone call.
LATIMER:	Well?
LAURA:	How do you know that call wasn't all part of a deliberate plan to involve you in this affair? After all, if you wanted to commit a murder what's the first thing you'd do?
LATIMER:	Provide myself with an alibi.
LAURA:	(*Nodding*) And the police with a possible suspect.
LATIMER:	You mean that Charles deliberately threw suspicion on to me in order to divert attention from himself? (*Shaking his head*) No, I can't believe that. If it was Charles that telephoned – and I believe it was in spite of what the Inspector says – there's a simple explanation for all this.
LAURA:	I hope you're right, Howard. That man you saw last night – Brady – did he mention Charles?

LATIMER:	No.
LAURA:	But he mentioned Frieda Veldon?
LATIMER:	Yes, I told you. He asked me what she looked like, and what she was wearing. He even asked me if I'd noticed her shoes.
LAURA:	(*Facing him; puzzled*) Why should he do that?
LATIMER:	(*Shaking his head with a little laugh*) I don't know. I can't imagine why. Look, Laura – don't you start worrying about all this, please, darling.
LAURA:	I shan't worry if you make me a promise.
LATIMER:	Well?
LAURA:	If anything else happens – even if it's only another phone call – go straight to Scotland Yard.
LATIMER:	Yes, darling, of course, I shouldn't dream of doing anything else. (*Irritated*) Why does everyone get the impression I'm covering things up the whole time? I've been perfectly straightforward about the whole business.
LAURA:	(*Facing him; with almost a smile*) Yes, Howard.

The doorbell rings. LATIMER goes and opens the door and KEN PALMER is standing there.

| LATIMER: | Why, hello, Ken! |

PALMER enters.

PALMER:	Morning, Squire! You forgot your electric razor.
LATIMER:	Oh, thanks very much. I was going to ring you about it.
PALMER:	I was passing so I thought I'd drop it in.
LATIMER:	You're up nice and early this morning.

71

PALMER: Yes, old boy. Golf. (*Surprised*) Why, hello, Laura!

LAURA: Good morning, Ken.

PALMER: How are you?

LAURA: I'm all right, thank you. And you?

PALMER: Oh, bearing up, you know, under the stress and strain.

LATIMER: What stress and strain? You've never done a day's work in your life!

PALMER: I know, old boy, that's what worries me. The way things are going I shall have to start.

LAURA: (*To LATIMER*) Darling, I must be off.

LATIMER: Yes, all right, Laura.

LATIMER and LAURA walk toward the door.

PALMER: Goodbye, Laura. Nice to see you again.

LAURA: Goodbye.

LATIMER and LAURA leave the room and close the door. A few moments later LATIMER returns alone.

PALMER: I say, I'm sorry if I barged in on anything.

LATIMER: You didn't.

PALMER: (*Grinning*) Really, old boy?

LATIMER: Just in case you have any unpleasant thoughts, Mr Palmer. My fiancée arrived here exactly half an hour ago.

PALMER: Does she usually pop in at this time of the morning?

LATIMER: No, she doesn't. She was worried about last night so she called round. I asked her to get me some breakfast.

PALMER: (*Who doesn't believe a word of it*) And a jolly good idea, Squire. Nothing like having a woman round the place. What was it old Bill Shakespeare said? "As for the women, though

72

	we scorn and flout 'em, we may live with but cannot live without 'em".
LATIMER:	That doesn't sound like Shakespeare to me. Sounds more like Ken Palmer.
PALMER:	You're probably right, doc. Anyway, she's jolly nice.
LATIMER:	(*After a moment, his thoughts elsewhere*) M'm?
PALMER:	I said she's jolly nice.
LATIMER:	Who?
PALMER:	Laura, Doc. Laura. Who do you think I'm talking about?
LATIMER:	(*Feeling his head*) I'm sorry, Ken. I'm a bit hazy this morning. I didn't sleep very well last night.
PALMER:	I can understand it. Didn't sleep much myself. (*A moment*) Howard, how's Laura taken all this?
LATIMER:	She's been pretty wonderful about the whole business. After all, you've got to look at it from her point of view. That girl – Frieda Veldon – was actually found here – in my flat.
PALMER:	(*Thoughtfully*) Yes, that must have been quite a blow.
LATIMER:	Of course it was a blow! (*Turning*) Ken, would you like some coffee?
PALMER:	No thanks, doc. I must be off. I'm supposed to be on the first tee by ten o'clock.
LATIMER:	(*Helping himself to another cup of coffee*) Where are you playing?
PALMER:	Royal Wimbledon. Oh, which reminds me, Doc – do you mind if I borrow that putter of yours? The one with the magic touch?

73

LATIMER: (*Smiling*) Help yourself – it's in the cupboard.
              But I don't guarantee the magic.

PALMER opens a cupboard door and takes LATIMER's putter from his golf bag.

PALMER: (*Gently swinging putter*) Ah, there you are,
              old girl. You know this isn't a putter, it's a
              magic wand. No wonder you always skin me
              alive!

LATIMER: The next time I skin you alive will be the
              first.

PALMER laughs.

LATIMER: I've bought you enough beer to float a
              battleship. Thanks for bringing the razor.

PALMER sits on the arm of the settee.

PALMER: Do you like those electric things?

LATIMER: Yes, I do, rather. They take a bit of getting
              used to. (*Feels his chin*) I used the old cut-
              throat this morning – I was terrified.

PALMER: You seem to have survived all right.
              (Ca*sually; picking up a biscuit off the tray*)
              Howard, you know that detective who called
              round last night?

LATIMER: Dane? Yes?

PALMER: How long have you known him?

LATIMER: Oh, about two or three days. Why?

PALMER: He seemed rather an odd chap, I thought.

LATIMER: What do you mean – odd?

PALMER: Oh, I dunno. He didn't look like a detective to
              me.

LATIMER: I can assure you he is one.

PALMER: Not my idea of a flat foot. Far too much of the
              gent.

LATIMER: What did you expect him to do – chew
              tobacco and wear a bowler hat?

74

PALMER:	(*Laughing*) No, but I didn't think they came quite as smooth as that. Do you know what his hobby is?
LATIMER:	No.
PALMER:	Bird watching.
LATIMER:	Who told you that?
PALMER:	He did.
LATIMER:	When?
PALMER:	Last night before you arrived. It was rather funny, when I got back from the party he was on the doorstep. I asked him who he was; he told me and said he wanted to see you. I tried to kid him along at first, pretending I'd never heard of you. It was just like water off a duck's back. He simply followed me into the flat.
LATIMER:	What made him tell you about his hobby?
PALMER:	I don't know. I expected him to ask me all sorts of questions about you – the murder – Charles Kaufmann. He didn't say a damn thing. Just sat smoking his cigar. Then suddenly, quite out of the blue, he said "Are you interested in bird watching, Mr Palmer?"
LATIMER:	(*Faintly amused*) What did you say?
PALMER:	Well, when I'd sorted out what he meant, I said no. What else could I say?
LATIMER:	Then what happened?
PALMER:	Well, he just went on talking about bird watching. (*A little laugh*) Most extraordinary chap.
LATIMER:	I wish to God he'd talk to me about bird watching. He's very much on the ball when I see him.
PALMER:	What happened after you left?

LATIMER:	I gave him a lift as far as Piccadilly.
PALMER:	(*Casually*) Did he mention me at all?
LATIMER:	No, why should he?
PALMER:	Well, I know you'll think I'm crazy, especially after what I've told you. But I had a funny feeling last night.
LATIMER:	What kind of feeling?
PALMER:	(*Vaguely*) Oh – it's difficult to explain. You'll probably think I'm quite mad.
LATIMER:	I've thought that for years, old boy – but go on.
PALMER:	Well, I got the impression it wasn't you he was interested in. It was me.
LATIMER:	You?
PALMER:	Yes.
LATIMER:	Why should he be interested in you?
PALMER:	I don't know.

LATIMER rises.

LATIMER:	(*Amused*) This sounds to me remarkably like a guilty conscience.
PALMER:	No, seriously, Doc.
LATIMER:	If he'd been interested in you he wouldn't have talked about bird watching, believe me.
PALMER:	(*Thoughtfully*) I don't know.
LATIMER:	Well, I do. He'd have talked about Ken Palmer, Esq., make no mistake about that. He'd have asked you all sorts of questions.
PALMER:	(*With a laugh*)I suppose you're right. Well, I must be off! It's all right, old boy. I can let myself out.
LATIMER:	Keep out of the rough!
PALMER:	I'll try. Cheerio.

PALMER goes out. LATIMER picks up the case containing the razor. He turns and looks towards the hall.

CUT TO: Hospital Consulting Room.

LATIMER enters and joins DETECTIVE INSPECTOR DANE who is already in the room.

DANE: (*Turning; pleasantly*) Good afternoon, doctor.

LATIMER: I understand you want to see me?

DANE: Yes. I'm sorry to disturb you, sir. (*Smiling*) I hope you can spare me a few minutes.

LATIMER: What is it you want?

DANE: (*Disarmingly*) If you'd prefer that I came back later, sir?

LATIMER: (*Relenting slightly*) No, no, that's all right. What is it?

DANE crosses to his case and opens it. He takes out a candlestick.

DANE: I want you to take a look at this, sir.

LATIMER looks at the candlestick.

LATIMER: Is that the candlestick you found in my car?

DANE: Yes, sir. (*Watching him*) Have you seen it before?

LATIMER: No.

DANE: You will notice the top half is missing. You haven't seen it by any chance, have you, Dr Latimer?

LATIMER: No, I haven't.

DANE replaces the candlestick in his case.

DANE: We found it in the boot of your car, sir. It was wrapped in a piece of oil cloth.

LATIMER: (*Looking at DANE*) Yes, you told me.

DANE: (*Nodding*) It's been through the Lab. They're quite satisfied. It's the weapon all right. (*He closes the case*) I suppose you've no idea how it got into the car?

LATIMER: No, I'm afraid I haven't. What about fingerprints?

77

DANE:	(*Shaking his head*) There was nothing. Nothing at all. (*He puts the case down on the floor and straightens himself*) Doctor, you remember what you told me about Mrs Frobisher?
LATIMER:	Yes.
DANE:	(*Slowly, as if remembering*) She told you her daughter found the body of a man in the grounds of a house called …
LATIMER:	'Heronswood'! According to Mrs Frobisher there was a brass candlestick by the body.
DANE:	Did she describe the candlestick?
LATIMER:	Yes, she said it had a twisted stem – like that one.
DANE:	(*A sudden thought*) Did her daughter – the little girl herself – confirm the story, sir?
LATIMER:	I didn't discuss it with her daughter.
DANE:	(*Faintly surprised*) You didn't?
LATIMER:	No.
DANE:	Why not?
LATIMER:	It was the first time I'd seen the child and I wanted to gain her confidence, to get to know her.
DANE:	Well, what did you discuss?
LATIMER:	We talked about squirrels.
DANE:	Squirrels?
LATIMER:	Yes.
DANE:	I see, sir.
LATIMER:	I doubt whether you do see, Inspector.
DANE:	I should feel a great deal happier if Mrs Frobisher and Dr Kimber would confirm your story, sir.
LATIMER:	So should I.

DANE: I might even feel happier if we could find the house.

LATIMER: Isn't there a house called 'Heronswood'?

DANE: (*Shaking his head*) Not in Hampstead. (*He looks at LATIMER for a moment and then suddenly picks up the attaché case*) Well – thank you, doctor.

DANE moves towards the door, then stops.

DANE: (*Smiling*) Oh, excuse my asking. What does your friend Mr Palmer do for a living?

LATIMER: He doesn't do anything. He studied medicine for eighteen months, then he went on the stage, then an aunt of his died and left him ninety thousand.

DANE: When was that?

LATIMER: About six months ago. He hasn't done a stroke of work since. Unless you call getting out of bunkers work.

DANE: (*Almost a sigh*) I can't honestly say I blame him, sir. You've known him quite a time, then?

LATIMER: Oh, yes. Since Medical School.

DANE: Is he a friend of Mr Kaufmann's?

LATIMER: They've met; I wouldn't call them friends.

DANE: (*Nodding; moving towards the door*) Well, he certainly plays the piano very well.

LATIMER: Yes, he does. (*Smiling*) He's also allergic to bird watchers.

DANE: (*With the suggestion of a smile*) I'll bear that in mind, sir. Good afternoon.

DANE goes out.

CUT TO: Shoe Shop.

JOYCE EDWARDS is behind the counter. LATIMER rushes in.

LATIMER: (*Smiling*) It looks as if I've just made it!

JOYCE: We're just closing, sir, but if there's anything I can do?

LATIMER: I've called for a parcel for Miss James. I believe it should have been picked up yesterday.

JOYCE: (*Smiling*) Oh, Miss James! Yes, of course. It's ready for her.

JOYCE finds the parcel beneath the counter and gives it to LATIMER.

LATIMER: Thank you.

JOYCE: They are paid for.

LATIMER: I'm relieved to hear it.

CUT TO: LATIMER's flat.

ROBERT BRADY closes a cupboard door and then goes into the bedroom. A few moments pass and then BRADY comes out of the bedroom and picks up the telephone and dials a number.

MAN'S VOICE: Hello?

BRADY: This is Brady. Look, there's something wrong. I've searched the place and it's not here.

MAN'S VOICE: Right, Brady, leave it.

BRADY: Where is Latimer?

MAN: He left the hospital half an hour ago.

BRADY: Half an hour ago? (*He looks at his watch*) He should be here by now.

MAN: He picked up a parcel from a shop in South Audley Street.

BRADY: (*Curious*) What kind of a shop?

80

MAN: A ladies' shoe shop.

BRADY: Wait a minute.

BRADY leaves the phone and crosses to look out of the window. He sees LATIMER arriving in a taxi. BRADY returns to the phone.

BRADY: He's just arrived. I'll contact you later.

BRADY puts down the phone. He takes a gun out of his pocket and points it as LATIMER enters.

LATIMER: (*Tersely*) What are you doing here?

BRADY: I should have thought that was obvious. I'm waiting for you. By the way, your phone's out of order.

LATIMER: What do you mean, it's out of order? (*Angrily*) Who are you?

BRADY: (*Quietly*) I told you who I am. I told you last night. I am a friend of yours.

LATIMER: (*Looking down at the revolver*) You look extremely friendly at the moment, I must say!

BRADY: I dislike this as much as you do, Dr Latimer.

LATIMER: Then why not dispense with it?

BRADY: Because if I did I have a shrewd suspicion you'd take advantage of me. (*He sits on the arm of the settee*) What happened last night?

LATIMER: I came back here, got the matches, and then someone knocked me out. When I returned to St John's Wood you'd disappeared.

BRADY: And the matches?

LATIMER: I don't know what happened to them. Whoever knocked me out must have taken them.

BRADY: Have you any idea who it was?

LATIMER: No.

81

BRADY: Well, you appear to have done your best, Dr
            Latimer. I'm grateful to you. Here's the
            photograph I promised you.

*BRADY takes the photo out of his pocket and puts it on the
table.*

LATIMER: I no longer need it.

BRADY: Why not?

LATIMER: The police believe my story. They know I
            went to the Airport.

BRADY: (*Interested*) Indeed?

LATIMER: Someone saw me.

BRADY: Who?

LATIMER: One of the nurses from the Mayfair Clinic.
            She was meeting a friend of hers.

BRADY: Did she see Windsor, too?

LATIMER: Yes.

BRADY: (*Smiling*) Still, you may keep the photograph
            – as a souvenir.

LATIMER: (*Not unfriendly*) Look, Brady, what is it you
            want? Why did you come here?

BRADY: Well, I should have liked the matches, Dr
            Latimer – but presumably you haven't got
            them.

LATIMER: No, I haven't.

BRADY: (*Slowly, smiling*) Well, in that case I'll take
            the parcel.

LATIMER: (*Surprised*) What parcel? What are you
            talking about?

BRADY: (*After a pause*) About half an hour ago you
            picked up a parcel. A pair of shoes.

LATIMER: (*Surprised*) Well?

BRADY: Where is it?

LATIMER: (*Puzzled*) It's in the hall.

BRADY: Would you mind getting it for me?

LATIMER:	(*Quietly, astonished*) Are you serious about this?
BRADY:	Perfectly serious.
LATIMER:	But why should you be interested in a pair of shoes that my fiancée ... (*He stops, stares at BRADY; a sudden thought has occurred to him*) Look here, now I come to think of it, you asked me about Miss Veldon's shoes.
BRADY:	Did I?
LATIMER:	Yes.
BRADY:	When?
LATIMER:	Last night: you asked me what kind of shoes she was wearing.
BRADY:	(*Shaking his head*) I don't remember.
LATIMER:	(*Curious*) You did.
BRADY:	(*Quietly*) If I did it was just a coincidence, I assure you. Get me the parcel, Dr Latimer.
LATIMER:	(*Watching BRADY*) How did you know I was going to pick up that parcel?

BRADY doesn't answer.

LATIMER:	Who told you about it? (*Curious*) Do you know my fiancée, Mr Brady? ... Well?
BRADY:	(*Politely, firmly*) Dr Latimer, please get me the parcel.
LATIMER:	Supposing I refuse? (*A moment*) Supposing I refuse to give you the parcel?
BRADY:	(*Quietly*) To say the least, it would prolong our conversation.

BRADY follows LATIMER out to the hall where LATIMER picks up the parcel off the table.

LATIMER:	I can't imagine why you want this, Brady – but you can have it with my compliments. On one condition.

BRADY: With all due respects, Dr Latimer, I hardly
            think that you're in a position to …

*LATIMER pretends to give the parcel to BRADY but instead
throws it at him using it as an opportunity to try to take the
revolver off of BRADY. They struggle. The gun goes off and
BRADY falls to the ground. LATIMER staggers back and
stares down at BRADY.*

CUT TO: *LATIMER in a telephone box. He is dialling a
number. We hear the number ringing out at the other end.*
MAN'S VOICE: Scotland Yard.
LATIMER: Put me through to Inspector Dane, please.
MAN'S VOICE: Who is it speaking?
LATIMER: My name is Latimer. Dr Latimer.
MAN'S VOICE: One moment, sir.
A pause. There is a 'click' on the switchboard.
LATIMER: (*Impatiently*) Hello? Hello?
A second pause.
DANE: (*On the other end*) Hello … Dane speaking …
LATIMER: (*Suddenly; quickly*) Inspector, this is Latimer.
            Come round to my flat immediately!
DANE: Why? What's happened?
LATIMER: There's been an accident.
DANE: What kind of an accident?
LATIMER: You remember that man I told you about –
            Brady?
DANE: Yes, I remember.
LATIMER: He was waiting for me when I got back from
            the hospital, he … Look, he's been shot –
            you'd better come round straight away.
DANE: I'll be there in fifteen minutes.
*LATIMER puts down the receiver and leaves the telephone
box.*

CUT TO: *LATIMER re-enters his flat. There is no sign of BRADY on the floor of the hall. LATIMER goes into the bedroom but he isn't there either. The telephone rings and LATIMER answers it.*

LATIMER: Hello? … Hello?

MAN's VOICE: (*On the other end*) Is that Sloane 1963?

LATIMER: Yes.

VOICE: Is that you, Howard?

LATIMER: (*Tensely*) Yes. Who is this?

VOICE: (*Surprised*) It's Charles, old boy!

LATIMER: (*Dazed*) Charles?

VOICE: Yes, Charles Kaufmann! Say, what happened to you, Howard? I tried to get you the other night and …

LATIMER: (*Interrupting him; tensely*) Charles, where are you? Where are you speaking from?

VOICE: I'm at the Savoy. Look, Howard – is anything the matter?

LATIMER: Yes, I've got to see you!

VOICE: Sure. Let's get together. How about lunch on Thursday?

LATIMER: No, you don't understand. This is urgent. Very urgent. I want to see you now, tonight.

VOICE: (*Seriously*) All right, come round here. I'll be in the bar.

LATIMER: No, no, I can't do that, Charles. I can't leave the flat.

VOICE: Well, what do you want me to do?

LATIMER: Jump in a cab and come round here now, straightaway.

VOICE: Straightaway?

LATIMER: Yes, it's very urgent. Please, Charles!

VOICE: (*A moment; then with a little laugh*) Okay! I'm on my way!

We hear the sound of the receiver being replaced at the other end. LATIMER replaces the receiver. He stands thinking, picks up a cigarette from the box, changes his mind, throws the cigarette back into the box and walks away from the table. He sees the parcel. He opens the box. It contains the top part of a brass candlestick.

END OF EPISODE THREE

EPISODE FOUR

OPEN TO: *LATIMER is looking at the parcel that contains the brass candlestick. He puts the parcel down on the table next to the case containing the electric razor. He looks puzzled and distinctly worried. He takes the candlestick out of the box and begins to examine it. The front doorbell rings. LATIMER looks up, hesitates, then replaces the candlestick in the box, and carries it to a side table near the radiogram. He goes out into the hall and opens the front door and LAURA JAMES enters.*

LATIMER: (*Surprised*) Hello, Laura! I didn't expect you so soon!

LAURA: I caught an early train.

LATIMER: (*Quietly*) Let me take your coat.

LAURA takes off her coat, looking up at LATIMER as she does so.

LAURA: Howard, is anything the matter?

LATIMER: Yes. (*Takes her coat and hangs it up*) I want to talk to you.

LATIMER and LAURA go through to the living room.

LAURA: (*Turning, anxiously*) What is it? What's happened? Have you seen the Inspector again?

LATIMER: Yes, he came to the hospital this afternoon but – (*Looks at LAURA*) That's not what I want to talk to you about.

LAURA: Well – what is it?

LATIMER hesitates; looks at LAURA for a moment.

LATIMER: Why didn't you tell me that you knew Brady?

LAURA: Brady?

LATIMER: Yes.

LAURA: You mean – the man you saw last night? The man that wanted the matches?

LATIMER: Yes.

89

LAURA: But I don't know him! What makes you think
            I do?

LATIMER: (*Quietly; facing her*) Laura, I want you to tell
            me the truth!

LAURA: (*A shade annoyed*) I am telling you the truth!

LATIMER: When I got back from hospital Brady was
            here; he was waiting for me.

LAURA: Well?

LATIMER: He knew about the shoes; he knew I'd been to
            the shop in South Audley Street.

LAURA: (*Bewildered*) The shoes? You mean, my
            shoes?

LATIMER: Yes.

LAURA: (*Shaking her head; confused*) Howard, I'm
            sorry. I don't understand this.

LATIMER: Brady asked me for the matches, when I said I
            hadn't got them he said he'd take the parcel
            instead.

LAURA: My parcel?

LATIMER: (*Almost irritated*) Yes, your parcel, Laura.

LAURA: But why on earth should he want … Did you
            give it to him?

LATIMER: No. (*Indicating the parcel*) It's over there.

*LAURA looks at LATIMER, hesitates, then crosses to the shoe
box. She sees the candlestick and is instinctively shocked, she
turns and stares at LATIMER in   astonishment.*

LAURA: (*Tensely*) Was this in the box the whole time?

LATIMER: (*Nodding*) It must have been.

LAURA: (*Still a shade tense; rigid*) Who opened the
            parcel?

LATIMER: I did.

LAURA: When?

*There is another pause. LATIMER is looking at his fiancée,
obviously puzzled.*

90

LATIMER: (*Quietly*) Brady had a gun. I threw the parcel
              at him. There was a struggle, and he was shot.
              I went outside to phone for the police, when I
              got back, he'd disappeared. It was then that I
              opened the parcel.

LAURA: (*Puzzled*) But why go outside to phone?

LATIMER: (*Indicating the telephone*) He told me my
              phone was out of order. I thought he'd
              tampered with it.

LAURA: And did he?

LATIMER: No, Charles Kaufmann called me just before
              you arrived.

LAURA: (*Astonished*) Charles!

LATIMER: Yes, he's staying at the Savoy. He should be
              here any minute now.

*LAURA looks at LATIMER in astonishment and obvious
delight.*

LAURA: But Howard, this is wonderful news! Why
              didn't you tell me this before? (*Puts her arm
              on his shoulder*) You'll probably find Charles
              will explain everything!

LATIMER: Will he, Laura? (*Moves back; a note of
              tenseness in his voice*) Will he explain why
              there's a candlestick in that box instead of a
              pair of shoes? Will he explain why Frieda
              Veldon was murdered? Why Mrs Frobisher
              lied to me about her daughter?

LAURA: (*A moment; her expression changing again*)
              Howard, why are you looking at me like that?
              Do you think I'm mixed up in this?

*LATIMER takes hold of LAURA's arm; draws her towards
him.*

LATIMER: Are you, Laura?

LAURA: No, of course not.

LATIMER:	Because if you are, tell me. Tell me now before Dane gets here.
LAURA:	(*Releasing herself*) What are you saying? Are you crazy, Howard? I'd never heard of Brady until you told me about him last night!
LATIMER:	(*Quietly*) Then what am I going to tell the Inspector?
LAURA:	What do you mean?
LATIMER:	(*Indicating the box*) About the parcel?
LAURA:	You must tell him the truth.
LATIMER:	That you asked me to pick it up for you?
LAURA:	Yes. Howard, don't you see, that parcel could have been changed – it could have been changed while you were outside phoning the police.
LATIMER:	By whom?
LAURA:	Well, obviously by Brady.
LATIMER:	But Brady was shot. The revolver went off while we were struggling!
LAURA:	Then where is Brady?
LATIMER:	(*Perplexed*) I don't know. I just don't know, Laura.
LAURA:	Did you examine him?
LATIMER:	No.
LAURA:	Why not?
LATIMER:	I completely lost my head and dashed down to the phone box.
LAURA:	Then how do you know he was dead?
LATIMER:	(*Agitated*) I don't; but if he wasn't he must have been very badly hurt.

LAURA looks at LATIMER for a moment.

LAURA:	(*Quietly*) Then how was he moved – and who moved him?

*LATIMER hesitates, then shakes his head and turns away; he
is perplexed and agitated.*

LAURA: (*After a moment*) Howard, the Inspector isn't
going to believe your story. You know that,
don't you?

LATIMER: (*Turning; 'on edge'*) Well, what do you
suggest? I took your advice, Laura! You said,
if anything happened – if it's only a phone
call – get in touch with the police.

LAURA: I'm not saying you didn't do the right thing,
Howard. I'm just saying they won't believe
you.

The doorbell rings. LATIMER turns towards the alcove.

LAURA: Is that Charles?

LATIMER: (*Looking at his watch*) It could be.

*LATIMER goes out into the hall and opens the front door.
DANE is standing in the doorway with two plain clothes men.*

DANE: Good evening, doctor.

LATIMER: Good evening.

*LATIMER stands to one side and DANE enters followed by
the two plain clothes men. LATIMER, DANE and one of the
detectives go into the living room. DANE is obviously
surprised to see LAURA.*

DANE: Hello, Miss James! I didn't expect to find you
here! (*He turns towards LATIMER*) Where's
Brady?

LATIMER: (*Hesitantly*) I'm afraid he's not here,
Inspector.

DANE: But you said he was here? You said there'd
been an accident – he'd been shot.

LATIMER: Yes, I know I did, but –

*DANE is walking round the room; his manner is casual, but
he might almost be looking for something.*

DANE: You shouldn't have moved him, sir.

LATIMER:	I didn't move him.
DANE:	(*Politely; without turning*) Then where is he?
LAURA:	I think you'd better tell the Inspector what happened, Howard.

DANE has reached the shoe box and sees the candlestick; he turns, looks at LATIMER, then slowly takes the candlestick out of the box.

DANE:	(*Quietly; looking at the candlestick*) Yes, I think you'd better, doctor.

CUT TO: As before.

DANE is sitting in the armchair holding the candlestick; LAURA is sitting opposite him with LATIMER by her side. The plain clothes men have departed. DANE looks at his watch.

DANE:	It doesn't look as if your friend Charles is coming.
LATIMER:	He said he was coming! He said he'd come straight away.
DANE:	That's over an hour ago, doctor. He should have been here by now.
LAURA:	(*To LATIMER*) Why don't you ring the hotel?
LATIMER:	(*After a moment's hesitation*) Yes, all right.

LATIMER crosses to the telephone and starts to dial a number. DANE rises.

DANE:	I think you're wasting your time, sir.
LATIMER:	(*Stops dialling; still holding the receiver*) What do you mean?
DANE:	I doubt very much whether Mr Kaufmann is staying at the Savoy.
LATIMER:	Of course he's staying at the Savoy, he … (*Replacing the receiver; angry*) You mean you don't believe me? You don't believe I received a phone call?

DANE: (*With the suggestion of a smile*) Dr Latimer, you have an irritating habit of putting words into my mouth. I didn't say I didn't believe you. I said I doubt very much whether Mr Kaufmann is staying at the Savoy.

LATIMER: (*Irritated*) Of course he's staying at the Savoy! I tell you he phoned me. He said he was coming straight here!

DANE: (*Patiently*) Then why hasn't he arrived?

LATIMER: (*Angry*) I don't know why!

LATIMER turns away from the table. The INSPECTOR looks across at LAURA.

DANE: Miss James, this shop in South Audley Street …

LAURA: Yes?

DANE: Have you ever been there before?

LAURA: No, I usually get my shoes from a shop in Kensington.

DANE: Then what made you go to 'Madeline'?

LAURA: I saw a pair of shoes in the window which I liked.

DANE: (*Looks at the candlestick*) I take it you were very surprised when Dr Latimer showed you the candlestick?

LAURA: Very.

DANE: (*With a smile at LATIMER*) Did you believe him?

LAURA: What do you mean?

DANE: Did you believe him when he told you that the candlestick was in the parcel?

LAURA: Yes, of course I believed him. I always believe my fiancé. In any case, I saw the candlestick for myself.

DANE: I see. Why didn't you pick up the parcel, Miss James?

LAURA: I told you. I've been out of town for the day; I only got back about an hour ago.

DANE: Yes, I understand that. But you bought the shoes yesterday.

LAURA: (*Nodding*) Yesterday morning. After I'd tried them on I realised I was late for an appointment so I said I'd pick the parcel up later.

DANE: But you didn't?

LAURA: No, I forgot all about it until this morning.

DANE: And then you asked Dr Latimer to pick it up for you?

LATIMER: Yes, that's right.

DANE looks at LAURA for a moment and then down at the candlestick.

LAURA: (*After a moment; looking at DANE*) Inspector, how well known was Frieda Veldon?

DANE: According to Dr Latimer, very well known.

LATIMER: I only repeated what Geoffrey Windsor told me: personally I'd never heard of her.

LAURA: (*Bluntly; facing DANE*) Was she a film star, Inspector?

DANE: (*Smiling; evasively*) You know, I always find the word 'star' faintly misleading. Nowadays every little actress seems to call herself …

LAURA: (*Interrupting him*) You know perfectly well what I mean. Was she a film star?

(*A moment*)

LATIMER: Well, Inspector?

DANE: (*A moment, then*) We'll know more about Miss Veldon tomorrow.

LATIMER: Why tomorrow?

DANE: Her brother's arriving from Berlin. Which reminds me. He may want to see you, Dr Latimer. If he does I should be very – discreet.

LATIMER: I'm making quite a feature of it these days, Inspector.

DANE smiles and moves towards the alcove.

DANE: Now, if you'll excuse me.

DANE reaches the alcove, then suddenly turns, hesitates.

DANE: Oh, there's something I've been meaning to ask you. Does the name Kroner mean anything to you?

LATIMER: Kroner?

DANE: Yes. Albert Kroner.

LATIMER shakes his head.

DANE: You've never heard of anyone called Albert Kroner?

LATIMER: (*Shaking his head*) No, I'm afraid I haven't.

DANE: (*Pleasantly*) He's not a patient of yours?

LATIMER: Well, if he was a patient I should have heard of him, shouldn't I?

DANE: (*Smiling*) Yes, of course. (*Moves towards the alcove again*) It's all right, sir. I can let myself out.

DANE goes out through the alcove. LAURA and LATIMER look towards the alcove. After a moment we hear the front door open and close. LATIMER turns towards LAURA.

LATIMER: Why did you ask him about Frieda Veldon?

LAURA: Because I've a feeling that the police know a great deal more about Miss Veldon than we do.

LATIMER: That wouldn't be difficult. I know nothing about her. Except that she was murdered and she was a friend of Charles'.

LAURA:	I wonder if she was a friend of Charles?
LATIMER:	What do you mean?
LAURA:	Supposing she wasn't a film star, Howard? Supposing she didn't come over here to make a film?
LATIMER:	(*Sitting on the arm of the settee; interested*) Go on, Laura.
LAURA:	Well, I was just thinking. Supposing Frieda Veldon and Brady and that man Windsor and the man the Inspector's just mentioned – what was his name?
LATIMER:	Kroner.
LAURA:	That's right. Albert Kroner. Supposing the whole lot of them were members of … (*Hesitates*)
LATIMER:	Members of what?

The doorbell is ringing.

| LAURA: | Well, of some political group or other. Isn't it possible that Frieda Veldon … (*Hesitates; looks towards the alcove*) that's the doorbell, Howard. |

LATIMER rises; turns towards the alcove. The doorbell rings again. LATIMER looks at LAURA, then quickly goes through the alcove to the hall. He opens the front door. DR GEORGE KIMBER is standing in the doorway. He looks worried and faintly agitated.

LATIMER:	(*Surprised*) Hello, George!
KIMBER:	Howard, I want to have a word with you. May I come in?
LATIMER:	Yes, of course.

KIMBER enters.

| KIMBER: | (*Taking off his gloves*) A man just passed in a car, who looked remarkably like Inspector Dane. |

98

LATIMER: (*Turning; closing the front door*) It was Dane.
              Come in, George.

*They go through to the living room. KIMBER is surprised to
find LAURA in the room. He looks at LATIMER, a shade
embarrassed.*

LATIMER: I don't think you've met my fiancée. (*To
              LAURA*) Darling, this is Dr Kimber.

KIMBER: (*Shaking hands with LAURA*) How do you
              do?

LAURA: (*Smiling*) How do you do, Dr Kimber? I've
              often heard Howard speak of you.

KIMBER: Howard, I didn't realise you had company,
              otherwise …

LATIMER: That's all right. What is it you want to see me
              about?

KIMBER glances across at LAURA and hesitates.

KIMBER: (*Forcing a smile*) It's not frightfully
              important. I'll give you a ring tomorrow.

LATIMER: No, don't be silly. It's obviously pretty
              important or you wouldn't be here.

LAURA: (*To LATIMER*) I'm just going to powder my
              nose, Howard. I'll be back in a few moments.

LAURA moves towards the bedroom.

LATIMER: No, wait, Laura! Your nose doesn't need
              powdering and what Dr Kimber's got to say
              can be said in front of you. (*To KIMBER*)
              Now come on, George – out with it.

KIMBER looks at LAURA again then turns to LATIMER.

KIMBER: (*Hesitantly*) Well – it's about Mrs Frobisher.

LATIMER: (*Interested*) What about Mrs Frobisher?

KIMBER: (*Agitated; still a shade reluctant to talk in
              front of LAURA*) I'm worried, Howard. Very
              worried.

LATIMER: So am I. That makes two of us. Now what is it, George? What is it you want to tell me?

KIMBER: When you told me about Mrs Frobisher, about the interview you had with her and the story she told you, I …

LATIMER: You didn't believe me.

KIMBER: No, I didn't. I thought you'd invented the whole thing.

LAURA: (*Indignantly*) Why should you think that? Why should Howard …

LATIMER: (*Stopping her*) Laura, please! (*To KIMBER*) Go on, George.

KIMBER: (*To LAURA*) Mrs Frobisher said nothing to me about a dead man, about her daughter suffering from hallucinations, the first I heard of it was when the Inspector spoke to me.

LATIMER: (*Quietly; watching him*) Go on, George.

KIMBER: Well, I've changed my mind.

LATIMER: Changed your mind – what about?

KIMBER: (*Faintly surprised by the question*) About you, Howard. I believe you. I think Mrs Frobisher did tell you that story.

LATIMER: This is very gratifying, George, but it's a little late in the day.

LAURA: It's a pity you didn't tell the Inspector that you believed Howard's story.

KIMBER: (*To LAURA; faintly irritated*) But I didn't believe it, not at first! That's what I'm trying to tell you.

LATIMER: (*Watching KIMBER*) Something's made you change your mind …

KIMBER: (*Quietly*) Yes.

LATIMER: Well – what is it?

KIMBER: On Saturday night I went out to dinner with a friend of mine. He's a Radiologist at the Queen Elizabeth in Birmingham. We went to a little restaurant in Kensington, and sitting almost opposite us was Mrs Frobisher. Well, to cut a long story short my friend recognised her. He said she was quite well known in the Midlands and was by way of being a notorious character. Naturally, I was very interested in all this and the following morning I decided to call round on Mrs Frobisher. To be frank, I thought I might be able to have a chat with the little girl. (*Shaking his head*) Ann Frobisher wasn't there. Her mother packed her off to Zurich two days ago.

LATIMER: (*Thoughtfully*) I see.

KIMBER takes out his cigarette case.

KIMBER: I thought you ought to know that, Howard.

LATIMER: (*Quietly; still thoughtful*) Yes. Yes, indeed. Thank you, George.

KIMBER offers LAURA his cigarette case but she shakes her head.

KIMBER: (*Feeling in his pocket*) If I were you I should have a word with the Inspector about it.

LAURA: Why don't you have a word with the Inspector, Dr Kimber?

KIMBER: (*Slightly irritated*) Well, it's hardly my business. Besides, I've got to be careful. Mrs Frobisher's still a patient of mine.

KIMBER offers LATIMER a cigarette but LATIMER refuses.

LATIMER: Did she see you, George – in the restaurant, I mean?

KIMBER: Yes. She nodded.

LATIMER: Who was she with?

KIMBER: Oh, a man I'd never seen before. Strange
             looking chap with glasses. (*Casually*) Have
             you a match, Howard?

*LATIMER crosses and picks up a lighter off the table; he
lights KIMBER's cigarette for him.*

LAURA: Did your friend say anything else about Mrs
             Frobisher?

KIMBER: No, but what he did say convinced me that he
             was telling the truth. It's quite obvious she's
             been a shady character, if she isn't one now.

LATIMER: You say her daughter's in Switzerland?

KIMBER: Yes, apparently she's staying with some
             friends in Zurich.

LAURA: (*To LATIMER*) It looks as if she got the child
             out of the way as quickly as possible.

KIMBER: Yes, that's exactly how it struck me.

LATIMER looks thoughtful.

LATIMER: (*Recovering his thoughts*) Well, thank you,
             George. Would you like a drink?

KIMBER: No. No, I must be off. I've an appointment at
             six o'clock. (*Turns, then hesitates*) There's
             just one point, Howard.

LATIMER: Yes?

KIMBER: Naturally, you'll tell the Inspector what I've
             told you, but – well – if you could keep my
             name out of it.

LATIMER: I don't see how I can.

KIMBER: Well, you can say you've heard that Mrs
             Frobisher isn't all that she makes herself out
             to be. You don't have to tell him how you've
             heard.

LATIMER: All right, George. We'll see.

KIMBER: Simply tell them to make inquiries about her, particularly in the Midlands. That should do the trick.

LATIMER nods.

LAURA: Who is this friend of yours, Dr Kimber? The one you had dinner with?

KIMBER: I told you. He's a doctor; a Radiologist. Well, I must be off. (*To LAURA*) Goodbye. So glad to have met you. I hope we shall meet again sometime.

LAURA: (*Coldly*) I hope so.

KIMBER hesitates, gives a little smile and then goes out followed by LATIMER. LAURA stands watching the alcove. We hear the front door open and close and LATIMER returns.

LAURA: I dislike that man, Howard! I dislike him intensely!

LATIMER: (*Smiling*) Yes, I rather thought you did.

LAURA: Do you believe his story?

LATIMER: Of course I believe it!

LAURA: Well, I don't! I think he had an ulterior motive in coming here this evening.

LATIMER: Laura, now don't be silly! How could he have an ulterior motive?

LAURA: Well, you can very easily find out.

LATIMER: How?

LAURA: Phone Mrs Frobisher and tell her you'd like to see her. Ask her point blank whether she lied to you about her daughter. Ask her whether Kimber is telling the truth about the girl being in Switzerland.

LATIMER looks at LAURA, hesitates, then makes up his mind to do as she suggests.

LATIMER: All right. All right, Laura.

LATIMER crosses to the bureau containing the telephone directories and picks up the E-K volume. He flicks through the pages. LAURA walks slowly up and down; thoughtful yet faintly agitated by the scene with KIMBER.

LAURA: You see, if you take the trouble to think about Kimber it just doesn't add up. In one breath he tells you that he doesn't want to be mixed up in this business, and in the next breath he tells you a story that he knows perfectly well is going to get him mixed up in it.

LATIMER: Yes, but he had to tell me about Mrs Frobisher. It was his duty to tell me.

LAURA: You think that's why he came here, Howard – because it was his duty? (*Shaking her head*) I don't like your friend Kimber. I don't trust him.

LATIMER: (*Looking at the directory*) Here it is. Hampstead 1962.

LAURA: And there's another thing, Howard. Don't forget it was Kimber that sent Mrs Frobisher to you in the first place.

LATIMER picks up the telephone and starts dialling.

LATIMER: Yes, but he didn't know she was going to tell me that story about the candlestick and the hallucination.

LAURA: How do you know he didn't? You've only his word for it. And how do you know it was an hallucination? Perhaps the child did find a dead body, perhaps she …

LATIMER: (*Interrupting; on the phone*) It's ringing.

A pause.

LATIMER: (*On the phone*) Hello? Is that Hampstead 1962?

GRACE: (*On the other end*) Yes.

104

LATIMER:	Can I speak to Mrs Frobisher, please?
GRACE:	Mrs Frobisher speaking.
LATIMER:	Oh, good evening. This is Dr Latimer.
GRACE:	Oh, good evening, Dr Latimer. I've been expecting you to call. I expect you've seen Dr Kimber.
LATIMER:	(*Surprised*) Yes, as a matter of fact he's just left.
GRACE:	What is it you want?
LATIMER:	I want to have a talk with you, Mrs Frobisher. Could we meet again sometime?
GRACE:	Is it urgent?
LATIMER:	Yes, I think perhaps it is.
GRACE:	(*Pleasantly*) Well, I'm dining in Town this evening. Why don't we meet beforehand, about half-past seven? Is that convenient for you?
LATIMER:	(*A shade taken aback by her pleasantness*) Yes.
GRACE:	Do you know 'The Pyramid'? It's a little restaurant in Kensington, just off Welford Street.
LATIMER:	I can find it.
GRACE:	All right, Dr Latimer. Half-past seven. Goodbye.

She replaces the receiver. LATIMER looks at the receiver he is holding and thoughtfully replaces it.

LAURA:	What did she say?
LATIMER:	(*Thoughtfully*) I'm seeing her tonight at half-past seven.
LAURA:	Where?
LATIMER:	At a restaurant in Kensington. 'The Pyramid'.
LAURA:	(*Nodding*) I've heard of it. It's just off Welford Street.

LATIMER:	That's right.
LAURA:	Was she surprised when you phoned?
LATIMER:	On the contrary, she seemed to be expecting me to ring. (*Turning towards Laura, collecting his thoughts*) Laura, I'd like you to come with me tonight. Is that possible?
LAURA:	Yes, I think so. (*Looks at LATIMER and nods*) It's probably a very good idea.
LATIMER:	Well, it'll give you a chance to form your own opinion of her, anyway. (*He picks up the case containing the electric razor*) I must confess she sounded very pleasant on the phone.
LAURA:	And not the notorious character Dr Kimber made her out to be?
LATIMER:	Still, Kimber must have been telling the truth. He wouldn't make up a story like that.
LAURA:	(*Moving towards the alcove*) Well, we'll see what Mrs Frobisher has got to say. I'm going home to change, Howard. I'll meet you at the restaurant at about twenty past seven.
LATIMER:	Yes, all right, Laura. Don't be late.

LAURA looks at him and smiles. LATIMER casually opens the case and takes out his electric razor. As he does so a piece of paper falls out of the case and on to the floor. LATIMER picks it up and unfolds it.

LAURA:	(*Casually*) What's that, Howard?
LATIMER:	I don't know. It dropped out of the case. (*He looks at the piece of paper and frowns*) That's damn funny.
LAURA:	What is it?
LATIMER:	(*Reading the note*) "Don't become too involved, Dr Latimer – or you'll regret it."

LAURA looks at LATIMER with surprise, then takes the note from him. She stares at it.

LAURA: (*Looking up*) This must be from Ken Palmer.

LATIMER: Why should Ken send me a note? He was here this morning. (*Shaking his head*) Anyway, it isn't his handwriting.

LATIMER takes the note back from LAURA and looks at it. He is obviously puzzled.

CUT TO: The living room in LATIMER's flat about half an hour later.

The room is deserted but someone is ringing the doorbell. LATIMER comes out of the bedroom wearing a dressing gown and crosses to the hall. We hear the front door open and the   sound of voices.

PALMER: (*Off*) Sorry if I've disturbed you, Doc!

LATIMER: (*Off*) Come in, Ken! I'm glad to see you.

KEN PALMER enters, followed by LATIMER. PALMER is on his way home from golf. His manner is the same as usual but as he talks he appears to be casually glancing around the room, as if looking for something. LATIMER notices this but makes no comment. PALMER's handkerchief is wrapped round the palm of his right hand.

PALMER: I was passing and I suddenly remembered I'm throwing a party tomorrow night and hadn't invited you and Laura.

LATIMER: That's very nice of you, Ken.

PALMER: Drop in any time after seven, Doc.

LATIMER: How did the golf go?

PALMER: The first round was a pip, an absolute pip, old boy. But this afternoon – ye Godfathers! I was in a bunker for twenty minutes. It's true, Doc. Cross my heart. The ruddy fool I was playing with had a stop-watch.

LATIMER: What's the matter with your hand?

PALMER: Oh, I couldn't get the car started and had to swing it. Caught the flipping thing on the radiator.

LATIMER: Let me have a look at it.

PALMER: No, it's nothing. Be all right when I've washed it. (*Smiling*) Do you mind if I use your bathroom?

LATIMER: No, of course not. Go ahead.

PALMER: Thanks.

PALMER crosses and goes into the bedroom. LATIMER stands looking towards the bedroom door, then he helps himself to a cigarette from the box on the table. He picks up the lighter.

LATIMER: (*Calling*) There's some iodine in the cupboard.

PALMER: (*Off*) Okay!

LATIMER lights his cigarette and puts down the lighter. PALMER returns from the bedroom: the handkerchief still wound round his hand.

LATIMER: All right?

PALMER: Yes; it's nothing.

LATIMER: (*Watching him; quietly*) Would you like a drink?

PALMER: No, thanks, old boy. I must hit the trail. I'm supposed to be going to a first night.

LATIMER: Ken, don't you ever get tired of first nights and parties and that sort of thing?

PALMER: (*A shrug*) Occasionally … It's a bit of a bind at times. (*Grins*) See you tomorrow, Squire.

PALMER crosses towards the alcove.

LATIMER: Yes, all right. (*A moment, then stopping him*) Oh, Ken …

PALMER: Yes?

108

LATIMER: (*A moment; changing his mind*) Seven
            o'clock you said?
PALMER: Yes, that's right. Anytime after seven.
            (*Smiles at Latimer*) Bye, Squire! (*He goes out
            through the alcove*)
*LATIMER looks towards the alcove; after a moment he takes
the note out of his dressing gown pocket and studies it. He
looks up and stares at the alcove.*

CUT TO: *A taxi drives up to 'The Pyramid' in Kensington.
LAURA gets out of the taxi and after paying the driver enters
the restaurant. The taxi driver puts up his flag, turns the cab
round, and drives away. The camera pans the taxi away from
the restaurant past a stationary car parked on the opposite
side of the road. A man is sitting in the car, he has watched
LAURA's arrival at the restaurant with interest. It is
GEOFFREY WINDSOR.*

CUT TO: A corner table in the restaurant.
*LATIMER is sitting at the table waiting for MRS
FROBISHER. There is a drink on the table. LATIMER rises
as LAURA arrives at the table.*
LAURA: Hasn't she arrived yet?
LATIMER: No. I've been here since a quarter past.
LAURA: I'm late. It's nearly twenty to.
LATIMER: Yes, I know.
They sit down at the table.
LAURA: (*Looking round the room*) This is rather nice.
LATIER: Yes. Would you like a drink, Laura?
LAURA: I think I would, darling. I'll have a sherry.
LATIMER: Ken Palmer called just after you left.
LAURA: (*Taking off her wrap*) Oh, did he?
LATIMER: Yes, he's asked us round for a drink
            tomorrow night.

LAURA: Is it a party?

LATIMER: I'm afraid so.

LAURA: Oh, dear! Do we have to go, Howard? Ken's
                parties are always so rowdy.

LATIMER: Yes, I know, but he's been pretty decent to
                me just recently and I don't want him to think
                … Anyhow, we'll see.

LAURA: Did you tell him about the note?

LATIMER: No.

LAURA: (*Surprised*) Why not?

LATIMER: (*Hesitant*) I don't know why not. I was going
                to tell him and then suddenly I – just changed
                my mind.

LAURA looks at LATIMER, obviously curious.

LAURA: Why?

LATIMER: I don't know why, Laura.

LAURA: You must have had a reason, Howard.

*Before LATIMER can reply a WAITER arrives at the table
carrying a note on a plate.*

WAITER: Dr Latimer?

LATIMER: (*Surprised*) Yes?

WAITER: … A note for you, sir.

*LATIMER takes the note off the plate and reads it. He looks
up at the WAITER.*

LATIMER: Who delivered this?

WAITER: A messenger boy, sir. He didn't wait, he said
                there was no reply.

LATIMER: (*Nodding*) Thank you. And bring my friend a
                glass of sherry, will you – dry sherry?

WAITER: Yes, sir.

The WAITER goes.

LAURA: What is it, Howard? Who's it from?

LATIMER: (*Quietly*) She's not coming.

LAURA takes the note and reads it. It says "Dear Dr Latimer, I'm very sorry but I can't see you tonight after all. Please phone me tomorrow. With apologies, Grace Frobisher."

LAURA: Why has she changed her mind, I wonder?

LATIMER takes the note from LAURA.

LATIMER: I don't know. She sounded quite friendly on the phone. (*Thoughtfully*) I wonder if someone was with her when I telephoned and that's why she said she'd meet ... (*He stops speaking and stares at the note*)

LAURA: (*Curious*) Howard, what is it?

LATIMER suddenly takes the first note out of his inside pocket – the one he discovered with the electric razor. He puts the two notes together on the table.

LAURA: (*Surprised*) It's the same handwriting!

CUT TO: Dr LATIMER's waiting room in Harley Street. The following afternoon.

LATIMER is sitting at the desk writing a letter. He finishes it, blots it and puts it in an envelope as NURSE KAY enters and crosses to the desk.

LATIMER: (*Handing her the letter*) I want Johnson to take this round to Dr Weston at the Clinic.

KAY: Yes, doctor.

LATIMER: Tell him not to wait for a reply. (*Opening the appointment book*) What time is my appointment with Lord Berkshire?

KAY: Half-past four; but there's a Mr Veldon to see you. I told him you couldn't see anyone without an appointment, but he seemed to think ...

LATIMER: (*Interrupting her*) Veldon?

The telephone rings on the desk.

KAY: Yes, sir.

The telephone continues to ring. LATIMER picks the receiver up and puts his hand over it; hesitates.

LATIMER: All right, I'll see Mr Veldon straight away. Show him up.

NURSE KAY goes out and LATIMER takes his hand off the receiver.

LATIMER: Hello?

LAURA: (*Other end*) Is that you, Howard?

LATIMER: Oh, hello, Laura! How are you?

LAURA: I've got rather a nasty headache, darling. I've had it all day. I don't feel a bit like going to a party.

LATIMER: Yes, all right, Laura. I'm not keen, anyway. I'll ring Ken and tell him we're not going.

LAURA: No, don't do that. He'll only think you don't want to go. Drop in for half-an-hour and then call round here.

LATIMER: Yes, all right, Laura.

LAURA: Have you spoken to Mrs Frobisher?

LATIMER: No, I've tried to get her two or three times but there's no reply. (*He looks up; his expression changes as NURSE KAY brings in VELDON*) I've got someone with me at the moment, Laura. I'll ring you back later. (*He puts down the receiver*)

KAY: Mr Veldon, doctor.

NURSE KAY goes out. VELDON slowly advances towards the desk. He is a dark, rather good-looking man in his late thirties. He wears a dark overcoat and carries a grey homburg hat. LATIMER rises and comes from behind the desk. VELDON looks at him for a moment before speaking.

VELDON: (*Unsmiling*) I apologise for intruding, Dr Latimer. Perhaps I should have made an appointment? (*His accent is slight and rather attractive*)

LATIMER: No, that's all right, Mr Veldon. Please sit down.

VELDON sits in the armchair and LATIMER leans against the desk.

VELDON: Thank you.

There is a slightly awkward pause.

LATIMER: When did you arrive?

VELDON: This morning. I left Berlin just after eight o'clock. I've been at Scotland Yard most of the day.

LATIMER: Does Inspector Dane know that you've called to see me?

VELDON: I told him I wanted to see you. (*Leaning forward slightly*) I want to know what happened, Dr Latimer.

LATIMER: What happened?

VELDON: That night – the night my sister was murdered.

LATIMER: I'm afraid I don't know what happened. I left her at Hyde Park Corner with a man called Geoffrey Windsor. He was supposed to take her to Claridges.

VELDON: (*Nodding; quietly, watching LATIMER*) Yes, the Inspector told me about Mr Windsor. Unfortunately, no one seems to have heard of him.

LATIMER: (*A shade tense*) Look, Veldon, I'll tell you everything I know, I'll answer any questions you like – but there's one thing I want to make quite clear. I did not murder your sister!

VELDON: (*Quite simply*) I have not said that you
              murdered her, Dr Latimer. (*After a moment*)
              Where did you first meet Frieda?
LATIMER: (*Surprised by the question*) At London
              Airport.
VELDON: You'd never seen her before?
LATIMER: No, never. To be frank, I'd never even heard
              of her.
VELDON: The Inspector said you went to the Airport
              because a friend of yours called Charles
              Kaufmann, is that right? …
LATIMER: Yes, that's right.
VELDON: … Asked you to meet my sister.
LATIMER: Yes, that's perfectly true.
VELDON: Why didn't Mr Kaufmann meet her himself?
LATIMER: (*Hesitant; a shade irritated*) I don't know
              why, at least … Well, he said he was in
              Scotland and couldn't get here in time.
VELDON: Is this Charles Kaufmann a friend of yours?
LATIMER: Yes, a very old friend. (*He sits on the arm of
              the other chair*) Didn't the Inspector explain
              about Charles; didn't he tell you what
              happened?

VELDON looks at LATIMER for a moment.

VELDON: (*Quietly*) Yes, he told me, Dr Latimer.
LATIMER: (*After a moment's hesitation*) Look, Veldon,
              I'm terribly sorry about your sister. Terribly
              sorry. Please believe me, if I could help you, I
              would.
VELDON: I think you can help me.
LATIMER: (*Puzzled*) How?
VELDON: I want you to tell me about your friend –
              Charles Kaufmann.
LATIMER: Why do you want to know about Charles?

VELDON: Because, according to the Inspector, that's
            why my sister came to England – to see Mr
            Kaufmann.

LATIMER: (*Surprised*) According to the Inspector?
            Didn't your sister tell you why she was
            coming here?

VELDON: She told me she was hoping to make a film,
            she didn't say who for.

LATIMER: You'd never heard of Kaufmann?

VELDON: Not until the Inspector mentioned him.

LATIMER: (*After a moment*) Veldon, I can understand
            your curiosity because I'm a little curious,
            too.

VELDON: About your friend?

LATIMER: No, about your sister.

VELDON: (*Puzzled*) So?

LATIMER: Tell me: was she a well-known actress?

VELDON: She played in one or two films and worked in
            a – what do you call it, repertory company?

LATIMER nods.

VELDON: But she was not a well-known actress, not a
            star.

LATIMER: Then why did Charles Kaufmann send for
            her? He's a well-known producer; he's made
            some very big films.

VELDON: I don't know why. I should like to know, Dr
            Latimer.

There is a pause.

LATIMER: Veldon, will you forgive me if I ask a
            personal question?

VELDON: If you have a question to ask, please ask it. I
            want us to be frank with each other.

LATIMER: Did your sister earn her living as an actress or
            had she – other interests?

VELDON: Other interests? I don't understand.
LATIMER: Was she entirely dependent on what she earned?
VELDON: Most definitely. Our parents died during the war. They were not wealthy people. What little money they left disappeared a long time ago.
LATIMER: I see.
VELDON: Occasionally, of course, I helped Frieda along. You know how it is. Things are difficult these days, especially in the entertainment business.
LATIMER: Are you in the entertainment business, Mr Veldon?
VELDON: No, no, God forbid! I'm an architect. I work for a firm called 'Muller and Vendenburg'. Our headquarters are at Hamburg, but I'm attached to the Berlin office.
LATIMER: I understand your sister lived in Berlin?
VELDON: That's right. We shared an apartment. Do you know Berlin, doctor?
LATIMER: No, I've never been there.
VELDON: And your friend, Mr Kaufmann, has he never been to Berlin?
LATIMER: (*Surprised by the question*) Well, I don't really know. He's been all over the place. I imagine he must have been there at some time or other.
VELDON: (*Nodding*) I see.
There is another uncomfortable pause, and then the door opens and NURSE KAY enters.
LATIMER: (*Relieved to see the NURSE*) Yes, what is it, Nurse?

116

KAY: Lord Berkshire's arrived, doctor. He's in the
            waiting room.

LATIMER: Oh! (*Nodding*) Thank you, Nurse. I'll ring.

NURSE KAY goes out, and VELDON rises.

VELDON: You mustn't keep your patients waiting, Dr
            Latimer. I won't detain you any longer.

LATIMER: How long are you staying in London?

VELDON: Until Tuesday morning. I'm at the
            Buckingham Hotel if you should wish to get
            in touch with me.

LATIMER: (*Turns and opens his appointment book*) I'll
            phone you tomorrow. We'll have another talk
            before you leave.

VELDON: (*Quietly*) Yes, I think perhaps it might be a
            good idea.

VELDON crosses to the door, then hesitates.

VELDON: Oh, before I forget, Dr Latimer, have you
            heard of a man called Albert Kroner?

LATIMER: (*Surprised*) Albert Kroner?

VELDON: Yes.

LATIMER: Yes, I have. The Inspector mentioned him last
            night. He asked me if I knew him.

VELDON: And do you know him?

LATIMER: No, I don't.

VELDON: (*Nodding*) The Inspector mentioned him to
            me this afternoon, just as I was leaving. He
            wanted to know if he was a friend of my
            sister's.

LATIMER: Was he?

VELDON: (*Shaking his head*) I don't think so. I don't
            ever remember Frieda mentioning the name
            Kroner. It's not a name you can very easily
            forget.

LATIMER: No, I suppose not.

117

VELDON: Did the Inspector say anything else to you about this man?

LATIMER: No, he just asked me if I knew him, that's all.

VELDON: (*Thoughtfully*) It's curious.

LATIMER: (*Puzzled*) Curious?

VELDON: Yes, it's curious that we've both never heard of him.

LATIMER: Why do you say that?

VELDON looks at LATIMER.

VELDON: I have a feeling they're very interested in Mr Kroner at Scotland Yard.

Suddenly, at LATIMER's astonishment, VELDON holds out his hand.

VELDON: Perhaps you'll telephone me, doctor – sometime tomorrow?

LATIMER: (*Shaking hands*) Yes, I will. Goodbye.

VELDON: Goodbye.

VELDON turns and walks towards the door. LATIMER watches him.

CUT TO: The front door of KEN PALMER's flat.

From inside the flat can be heard the sound of a party in progress; voices and general laughter. LATIMER arrives. He is wearing a light overcoat and carries his hat. He presses the bell push and stands waiting for the door to be opened. There is a pause, during which the noise of the party continues, but the bell remains unanswered. LATIMER smiles; presses the button again, and waits. After a moment, and somewhat amused, he presses the button once again. There is no answer. LATIMER hesitates, then keeps his finger on the button and knocks on the door with his free hand. There is still no reply. The noise of the party continues. LATIMER gives a shrug and turns away from the door; suddenly he remembers something, stops, feels in his waistcoat pocket. He

118

produces the key which KEN PALMER gave him; with a smile he inserts the key in the lock and lets himself into the flat. He goes into the hall closing the door behind him and crosses to the entrance to the drawing room. Suddenly he stops dead; an expression of complete surprise on his face. The room is empty of people. A gramophone record of party noises and chatter is being played. LATIMER slowly advances towards the radiogram. He switches off the record, then turns and sees the body of VELDON lying on the carpet in front of the settee; there is a revolver in his hand. After a moment of complete astonishment, LATIMER crosses and kneels down beside VELDON in order to examine him.

CUT TO: The outside of KEN PALMER's block of flats in St John's Wood.
Two Flying Squad Police cars race up to the entrance of the flats and brake to a standstill. A collection of uniformed and plain clothes men pour out of the cars. DANE is in the foreground, and is obviously in charge of operations. He stands on the pavement issuing urgent instructions to his men, instructing them to take up various positions in and near the block of flats.

CUT TO: The drawing room of PALMER's flat.
LATIMER rises from his position near VELDON, having completed his examination. He stands for a moment, staring down at the dead man, obviously worried and confused. Suddenly, he realises what a serious and incriminating position he is in, and quickly turns towards the hall. He flings open the door and finds himself face to face with DANE, and two plain-clothes men. He stops dead. DANE looks at him, takes him by the arm, and quietly leads him back into the drawing room. DANE crosses and immediately examines the body of VELDON. He shows no sign of surprise that

119

VELDON is in the flat. LATIMER stands watching DANE, and the two plain clothes men on either side of him. After a moment DANE rises, and nods to one of his men.

DANE: He's dead. Tell Findley I want him and contact the Lab.

One of the plain clothes men nods and goes out. DANE looks at LATIMER, at the body of VELDON, then at the DOCTOR again.

LATIMER: (*Tensely*) I know what you're thinking, Inspector. But you're wrong!

DANE looks at LATIMER, and for the first time there is a suggestion of anger in his voice.

DANE: Why did you lie to me?

LATIMER: (*Puzzled*) What are you talking about?

DANE: I asked if you knew this man. You said you'd never heard of him.

LATIMER: (*Pointing; astonished*) This man?

DANE: Yes, this man! You know as well as I do, this is Kroner. Albert Kroner!

END OF EPISODE FOUR

EPISODE FIVE

OPEN TO: KEN PALMER's flat.

DETECTIVE INSPECTOR DANE and LATIMER are standing over the lifeless body of ALBERT KRONER.

DANE: Why did you lie to me?

LATIMER: (*Puzzled*) What are you talking about?

DANE: I asked if you knew this man. You said you'd
            never heard of him.

LATIMER: (*Pointing; astonished*) This man?

DANE: Yes, this man! You know as well as I do, this
            is Kroner. Albert Kroner!

LATIMER: Albert Kroner?

DANE: (*Watching him*) Yes.

LATIMER: But this man came to see me this afternoon;
            he told me his name was Veldon, he said he
            was Frieda Veldon's brother.

DANE: Where did he see you?

LATIMER: At my rooms in Harley Street.

DANE: At what time?

LATIMER: Oh, about four fifteen.

DANE: Did anyone else see him?

LATIMER: Yes, Nurse Kay saw him, he told her his
            name was Veldon. That's the only reason I
            agreed to see him.

DANE looks at LATIMER.

LATIMER: Look, Inspector, I don't understand this.
            (*Points to Kroner*) He actually asked me if I
            knew Kroner, he said you'd questioned him
            about a man called Albert Kroner.

DANE looks at LATIMER with interest; his manner changes slightly; not quite so friendly.

DANE: All right, let's have the rest of the story.

LATIMER: Well – Ken Palmer told me he was giving a
            party. He invited my fiancée and I. When I
            arrived here there was a devil of a noise going

on and I couldn't make anyone hear. Suddenly, I remembered I had a key to the flat. Ken gave it to me the night I stayed here. I opened the door and let myself in. (*Nods towards the body*) This is what I found.

DANE: Where was the noise coming from?

LATIMER crosses, puts on his gloves and switches on the radiogram; he plays the record for a moment or two, and then stops the machine.

DANE: (*Nodding*) All right, so far, so good. But, where's Miss James?

LATIMER: She didn't come.

DANE: No? Why not?

LATIMER: She had a headache; she phoned me this afternoon and said she didn't feel like going to a party.

DANE: And Mr Palmer?

LATIMER: (*Shaking his head*) I don't know where Ken is.

A POLICE PHOTOGRAPHER enters and, completely ignoring the INSPECTOR and LATIMER, proceeds to take flash-light photographs of the body)

DANE: Dr Latimer, do you know why I came here this evening?

LATIMER: No, I'd certainly like to know.

DANE: Just over twenty minutes ago, a man telephoned my office, and asked me if I was interested in a certain Mr Albert Kroner. When I said I was, he suggested I visited this flat, without delay.

LATIMER: Who was this man?

DANE: (*Shaking his head*) I don't know, he didn't give his name, before I could question him he rang off.

124

The PHOTOGRAPHER has finished; he nods to DANE, and goes out.

LATIMER: Inspector, who is Kroner, anyway? Why are you interested in him?

DANE: We're interested in him for a number of reasons, Dr Latimer – but, let's just say he was a friend of Miss Veldon's.

As DANE finishes speaking, KEN PALMER bursts into the room, followed by a plain-clothes DETECTIVE.

PALMER: What is this? What the hell's going on around here? There's half Scotland Yard downstairs!

DETECTIVE: (*To DANE*) I'm sorry, sir. We couldn't stop him, he insisted on coming up.

PALMER: Of course I insisted on coming up! Don't be a clot, I live here!

DANE: (*To DETECTIVE*) That's all right, Lawson.

The DETECTIVE goes out, and KEN PALMER moves towards DANE and LATIMER.

PALMER: Now what is all this? Why on earth is the place ... (*He stops speaking; stares at the body of Kroner in astonishment*) Who – who's this?

DANE: (*Quietly; watching him*) Don't you know, Mr Palmer?

PALMER walks slowly round the settee, staring down at the body.

PALMER: No ... No, I don't. I've never seen him before. (*To LATIMER*) Is he dead?

DANE: Yes.

PALMER: (*Looks up at DANE*) Well – what's he doing here? How did he get into my flat?

DANE: We were hoping you'd be able to tell us that, sir.

PALMER:	(*Apparently stunned*) I don't know how he got in here; I haven't the slightest idea, I … (*To DANE*) Who is he?
DANE:	His name's Kroner.
PALMER:	Kroner?
DANE:	Yes.
PALMER:	(*Shaking his head*) I've never even heard of the man. (*Confused; to DANE*) What the hell is he doing here? (*He stares down at KRONER*)
DANE:	(*Quietly*) What happened to the party, Mr Palmer?
PALMER:	(*Looking up*) Party?
DANE:	Yes. Dr Latimer told me you were giving a party this evening.
PALMER:	So I was – (*Looks at LATIMER*) – until I got your telegram.
LATIMER:	My telegram?
PALMER:	(*Frowning*) Yes.
LATIMER:	What are you talking about?

DANE looks at PALMER, and across at LATIMER. PALMER takes a telegram out of his pocket and offers it to LATIMER. Before LATIMER can take it, the INSPECTOR stretches out his hand and takes the telegram. DANE looks at it. The camera pans in so that we can read what it says. The telegram, which was handed in at a Guildford post office at 2.35, is addressed to KEN PALMER, and reads as follows: "PLEASE CANCEL PARTY. MEET ME AT PICCADILLY HOTEL, GUILDFORD, SIX O'CLOCK TONIGHT. URGENTLY NEED YOUR HELP. HOWARD".

DANE:	(*To PALMER*) When did you receive this?
PALMER:	This afternoon, about four o'clock. Put me in a complete flap. I had a hell of a time putting people off.

126

DANE: Did you go to Guildford?

PALMER: Yes, of course I did! I've just got back from there. There isn't a ruddy Piccadilly Hotel!

LATIMER takes the telegram from DANE and reads it.

LATIMER: But I didn't send this, Ken!

PALMER: You didn't?

LATIMER: Of course I didn't.

PALMER: (*A shade angry*) Then who did? Somebody sent it!

DANE: (*Quietly*) That's just what I was thinking, Mr Palmer.

DANE looks across at LATIMER, then across to PALMER.

CUT TO: The living room of LATIMER's flat. Next morning.

The doorbell is ringing and LATIMER comes out of the bedroom and crosses to the alcove. He is fully dressed, except he wears a dressing gown, instead of his jacket. He opens the front door to reveal MRS FROBISHER, her hand still on the bell push. She looks worried and a shade agitated. LATIMER is surprised by the identity of his visitor.

GRACE: Good morning, Dr Latimer. I apologise for calling so early, but – could you spare me a few minutes?

LATIMER: Why, yes, certainly, Mrs Frobisher! Come in.

MRS FROBISHER enters and LATIMER closes the door. They go through to the living room. MRS FROBISHER puts her gloves and handbag down on the arm of the settee.

LATIMER: I'm sorry you had to cancel our appointment the other evening.

GRACE: Yes, I really ought to have phoned you, but – (*Anxiously*) – You did get my note?

LATIMER: Yes. Yes, I did indeed.

127

There is a slight pause. GRACE FROBISHER is obviously a shade embarrassed.

LATIMER: What is it you want to see me about?

GRACE: Why did you phone me – was it because of something Dr Kimber said?

LATIMER: Partly, and partly because I thought it was about time we had a little chat.

GRACE: (*Quietly; not looking at him*) Yes, I'd been expecting to hear from you. (*Turning towards him*) What did Dr Kimber say about me?

LATIMER: Supposing we forget Dr Kimber for a moment, and concentrate on what you told Inspector Dane.

GRACE doesn't reply.

LATIMER: You lied to the Inspector, Mrs Frobisher.

GRACE: (*A moment; nodding*) Yes.

LATIMER: Why?

GRACE: (*Anxiously; a shade tense*) Dr Latimer, tell me, what did Kimber say?

LATIMER: (*After a moment*) He said he'd seen you in a restaurant. He was having dinner with a friend and apparently his friend recognised you.

GRACE: (*Interested*) Who was this friend?

LATIMER: A doctor; a Radiologist from Birmingham. He said you were – quite well known in the Midlands.

GRACE: What did he mean – quite well known?

LATIMER: He implied that you had a bad reputation.

GRACE looks at LATIMER for a moment, and then gives a little smile.

GRACE: Is that all Kimber told you?

LATIMER: Isn't that enough?

GRACE's manner has changed slightly; she is still tense, but obviously not quite so worried.

GRACE: Dr Latimer, the story I told you about my daughter – about the dead man – the brass candlestick … (*shakes her head*) It wasn't true.

LATIMER: (*Angry*) Then why did you tell me it?

GRACE: I had to because … (*Hesitates*)

LATIMER: Well?

GRACE: I didn't realise what I was doing. I didn't realise that by telling you that story I was … throwing suspicion on to you …

LATIMER: You didn't throw suspicion on to me, but by not confirming what I told the Inspector, you gave the police the impression I was lying. That didn't help matters.

GRACE: I'm sorry, I didn't mean to do that, honestly I didn't.

LATIMER: Well, what did you mean to do? You knew you were lying. You must have had a reason for it.

GRACE: (*A moment*) Yes, I had a reason.

LATIMER: Well – what was is?

GRACE: I'm sorry – I can't tell you that.

LATIMER: You mean you can't – or won't – which is it?

GRACE: Look, Dr Latimer, I'm sorry for what I did. I apologise and I'd like to make amends for it.

LATIMER: There's only one way you can make amends.

GRACE: You mean by going to the Inspector and …

LATIMER: (*Nodding*) By going to the Inspector and telling him that you did tell me that story about your daughter and the brass candlestick.

GRACE looks up at LATIMER, undecided; suddenly, she makes up her mind.

GRACE: All right. (*Nodding; tensely*) All right, I'll do that, I promise you.

129

LATIMER: (*Quietly*) And you'll tell him why you told me
                the story?
GRACE: (*A shade tense; nervous*) No. No, I'm sorry, I
                can't do that. It's not possible.
LATIMER: Then you know as well as I do, the Inspector
                will think I've forced you into this. It's no
                use, Mrs Frobisher. You not only have to
                admit that you did lie, you've got to tell them
                why you lied in the first place.

*GRACE looks at LATIMER for a moment and then turns
away.*

GRACE: I'm sorry, Dr Latimer. I can't.
LATIMER: Then you can't help me.

*GRACE hesitates, then picks up her gloves and handbag off
the settee and moves towards the alcove. LATIMER watches
GRACE, then suddenly speaks.*

LATIMER: Mrs Frobisher.
GRACE: (*Stopping*) Yes?
LATIMER: Did Kimber know that you were going to tell
                me that story?
GRACE: (*Tensely; unable to conceal a note of
                desperation in her voice*) I can't answer that.
                (*Turning*) I'm sorry, Dr Latimer, I'd like to
                help you but ... (*With a sudden flash of
                anger*) I've told you, I'll go to the police and
                tell them I lied. I can't do more than that!

*LATIMER, tense and angry, crosses and takes hold of
GRACE's arm.*

LATIMER: You can do a great deal more! You can tell
                them the truth about this business, the whole
                truth.
GRACE: Leave go of my arm!
LATIMER: Mrs Frobisher, why did you tell me that
                story?

GRACE: Dr Latimer, please leave go of my arm!
LATIMER looks at her, hesitates, then releases her arm.
LATIMER: (*Quietly*) I'm sorry.
GRACE: (*After a moment*) Let me know if you change
             your mind, and you'd like me to speak to the
             Inspector. (*She crosses towards the alcove*)
LATIMER: No, please – wait a minute.
GRACE turns; a pause.
GRACE: Well, what is it?
LATIMER: You remember that note you sent me the
             other night.
GRACE: Yes?
LATIMER: Did you write it yourself?
GRACE: Why, yes, of course.
LATIMER: Then that wasn't the first note you sent me.
GRACE: What do you mean?
LATIMER: I found a note with my electric razor, it was in
             your handwriting. It said: "Don't become too
             involved, Dr Latimer – or you'll regret it".
GRACE: (*Facing LATIMER*) I know nothing about that
             note. But it's very good advice. If I were you,
             I should take it, Dr Latimer.

*GRACE FROBISHER goes out through the alcove. LATIMER
moves as if to stop her then changes his mind. He looks
worried, and a shade angry; he is also not at all certain that
he has done the right thing in letting her go. Suddenly, he
turns, picks up the telephone, and dials. There is a pause,
after he has finished dialling.*

LATIMER: (*On phone*) I want to speak to Dr Kimber …
             Well, please tell him it's urgent … This is Dr
             Latimer (*A pause*) George? This is Howard
             … Listen, I've got to see you; no, sometime
             this morning … That's no use, be here at my
             flat at twelve o'clock … (*Angry*) Well,

131

cancel it, this is important, too! … Twelve o'clock, George. (*He replaces the receiver before KIMBER can reply*)

LATIMER picks up a cigarette out of the box on the table, lights it, and then crosses to the bedroom; before he gets there, the telephone starts to ring. He hesitates, makes up his mind to ignore it, then changes his mind, and returns to the table, and picks up the receiver.

LATIMER: (*On phone*) Hello?

CUT TO: *GEOFFREY WINDSOR is holding a telephone receiver in a London call box. He suddenly presses button "A".*

WINDSOR: Dr Latimer? … This is Geoffrey Windsor … (*Smiling*) Yes, you've got the name right, doctor … No, don't ring off, I've got something to tell you. (*A moment*) Do you know "The Matador", it's a coffee bar in Knightsbridge? … Yes, that's right, that's the one … Well, I suggest you meet me there this morning at eleven o'clock … (*A moment, smiling*) For coffee, Dr Latimer … I'll tell you when I see you … I wouldn't do that if I were you, doctor – this concerns your fiancée … (S*lowly*) I'll tell you when I see you.

WINDSOR smiles and replaces the receiver.

CUT TO: Outside of 'The Matador' Coffee Bar.

'The Matador' is situated in a busy part of Knightsbridge; cars, pedestrians, etc. and on the pavement facing the entrance to the coffee bar are a group of buskers complete with musical instruments, hurdy-gurdy, etc. The chief busker is a tall man with a top hat, tail-coat, and tambourine. They are playing a popular tune of the moment.

132

A taxi drives up to the pavement and LATIMER gets out and turns to pay the driver. One of the buskers turns the hurdy-gurdy so that it points towards LATIMER and the chief busker crosses to LATIMER and flourishes his tambourine. LATIMER turns from paying the taxi driver, tries to ignore the busker, finally capitulates and drops a coin into the outstretched tambourine and crosses to the coffee bar.

CUT TO: Interior of the Coffee Bar.

LATIMER enters, looks round and notices GEOFFREY WINDSOR sitting alone at a corner table stirring a cup of coffee. He crosses to the table and stands looking at WINDSOR.

WINDSOR: (*Looking up*) You're late, Dr Latimer.

LATIMER: (*Curtly*) What is it you want?

WINDSOR: (*Smiling*) I want you to sit down.

LATIMER hesitates then sits down facing WINDSOR who picks up the menu.

WINDSOR: Can I interest you in a Kentucky Speciality?

LATIMER: I very much doubt whether you can interest me in anything. Now if you've got anything to say to me, please say it. I'm a very busy man.

WINDSOR: (*Quietly; still smiling*) And an impetuous one.

LATIMER: (*Angry*) What is it you want?

WINDSOR takes a drink and looks at LATIMER over the rim of his cup.

WINDSOR: (*Quite simply*) Four thousand pounds.

LATIMER: (*Staggered*) Are you serious?

WINDSOR: Perfectly serious.

LATIMER: Why should I give you four thousand pounds – why should I give you four thousand pence if it comes to that?

133

WINDSOR:	(*Putting down his cup*) Who said anything about <u>you</u> giving me four thousand pounds? You asked me what I wanted. I told you.
LATIMER:	Look, Windsor, suppose you stop talking in riddles and get to the point. If there is a point.
WINDSOR:	(*Smiling*) Oh, there's a point. (*A moment*) You have a friend – Dr Kimber.
LATIMER:	(*Quietly, surprised*) Yes?
WINDSOR:	I'd like you to see Dr Kimber and deliver a message for me.
LATIMER:	Why don't you deliver the message?
WINDSOR:	Because I should prefer you to do it, Dr Latimer.
LATIMER:	What is this message?
WINDSOR:	(*Quietly; business-like*) Tell him, I want four thousand pounds and I want it by Friday afternoon. Tell him that if he doesn't hand over the money to you by Friday, I shall send a letter to Inspector Dane.
LATIMER:	(*Puzzled*) A letter?
WINDSOR:	Yes. Just deliver the message, doctor. Kimber will understand.
LATIMER:	What do you know about Kimber?
WINDSOR:	(*A shrug*) Oh, so many things. He was a friend of Albert Kroner's.
LATIMER:	Kimber was?
WINDSOR:	Yes. (*Amused*) Didn't you know that?
LATIMER:	(*Annoyed*) Deliver your own message, Windsor! This is blackmail. I'm not getting mixed up in this.

WINDSOR: (*Ignoring LATIMER's remark*) I'll phone you on Friday. If you've got the money we'll arrange to meet.

LATIMER: (*Angry, rising*) You heard what I said, I'm having nothing to do with this!

WINDSOR: (*Quietly; self-possessed*) Sit down.

LATIMER looks at WINDSOR for a moment and then sits. A WAITRESS arrives at the table.

WAITRESS: (*To LATIMER*) Can I get you anything, sir?

LATIMER: (*Abruptly*) No.

WINDSOR: (*To WAITRESS*) Bring the gentleman a cup of coffee.

WAITRESS: Yes, sir.

The WAITRESS goes.

WINDSOR: Dr Latimer, tell me, just out of curiosity; do you think your fiancée was telling the truth about the parcel and the candlestick?

LATIMER: (*Tensely; obviously worried*) You leave my fiancée out of this!

WINDSOR: (*Nodding*) I should like to. It would be much pleasanter all round if we could leave her out of it.

LATIMER: What do you mean?

WINDSOR: (*Quietly; quite pleasant*) I've asked you to do something for me. If you do it there's absolutely no necessity for me to discuss Miss James with you, Inspector Dane, or anyone else.

LATIMER: And supposing I don't do it?

WINDSOR: (*A moment; watching LATIMER*) I think you will. You're no fool, doctor. And unless I'm very much mistaken you're very fond of that fiancée of yours. (*He rises, and nods*) I'll phone you on Friday.

135

WINDSOR leaves the table. LATIMER stares after him, puzzled and obviously worried. The WAITRESS arrives and puts the cup of coffee down on the table.

CUT TO: LATIMER's flat.
The doorbell is ringing. NURSE KAY comes out of the bedroom carrying a duster and crosses to the front door. She admits DR KIMBER.

KIMBER: (*Brusquely*) I have an appointment with Dr Latimer.

KAY: Oh – well, he's not here at the moment, doctor. But he shouldn't be very long. He's got an appointment in Harley Street at half past twelve.

KIMBER: He's got an appointment at twelve, here, with me.

KAY: Oh – well, er …

KIMBER: (*Looking at his watch*) I've cancelled two appointments to get here on time.

KAY: When did Dr Latimer make this appointment, doctor?

LATIMER enters the room from the alcove, he is wearing his coat and hat.

KIMBER: He phoned me this morning and said it was extremely urgent. If I'd known he was going to keep me waiting … (*Breaks off on seeing LATIMER*)

LATIMER: (*Taking off his hat and coat; to Kay, pleasantly*) Good morning, Kay.

KAY: I've tidied the bedroom and done most of the dishes, doctor.

LATIMER: Thank you very much, Kay. It's very kind of you. I'll do the same for you when you lose your housekeeper.

136

The NURSE gives LATIMER a look and picks up her hat and coat off the settee.

LATIMER: When you get back to Harley Street would you phone Miss James for me? Ask her to call here any time after four o'clock.

KAY: You've got Mr Stewart at three forty-five.

LATIMER: (*Nodding*) In that case make it any time after five.

KAY: Yes, doctor. (*A sudden thought*) Oh – I've brought the Duncan X-ray, it's on the table.

LATIMER: Thank you, Nurse.

KAY: Good-bye.

LATIMER: Good-bye.

KAY: Good-bye, Dr Kimber.

KIMBER: Good-bye.

NURSE KAY goes out through the alcove.

KIMBER: (*Irritated*) Howard, I've had to cancel two appointments to get here this morning. What is it you want to see me about?

LATIMER: Sorry I'm late, George, but I've been having coffee with a friend of yours.

KIMBER: A friend of mine?

LATIMER: Yes.

KIMBER: Who do you mean? (*A sudden thought*) Oh, Mrs Frobisher!

LATIMER: (*Shaking his head*) No, George. Not Mrs Frobisher. A gentleman called Geoffrey Windsor.

KIMBER: (*Obviously shaken*) Geoffrey Windsor?

LATIMER: Yes.

KIMBER: (*Shaking his head, but not very convincing*) I don't know anyone called Windsor.

LATIMER: Well, he seems to know you, George. He seems to know a great deal about you.

137

KIMBER: (*After an awkward pause*) When did you see Windsor?

LATIMER: I told you. This morning. I had coffee with him. Interesting man, Mr Windsor – full of interesting propositions. The sort of man you instinctively underrate. Did you underrate him, George?

KIMBER: What the hell are you talking about?

LATIMER: (*Suddenly; turning on KIMBER and taking him by surprise*) I'll tell you what I'm talking about! I'm talking about murder. The murder of Frieda Veldon and Albert Kroner.

KIMBER looks at LATIMER then turns away, he is obviously very shaken.

LATIMER: Did you kill Frieda Veldon?

KIMBER: No. I never even saw the girl.

LATIMER: And Kroner?

KIMBER: I knew Kroner, but – (*Tensely; facing LATIMER*) I didn't murder him, Howard. I swear I didn't.

LATIMER: That's not what Mr Windsor thinks.

KIMBER: Did Windsor mention Kroner?

LATIMER: He did. He did indeed.

KIMBER: How long have you known Windsor?

LATIMER: About a week. He came to interview me, he said he was a newspaper reporter. I believed him. In those dim and distant days I believed everybody, George. I've learnt my lesson since.

KIMBER: (*Quietly*) Is that why you sent for me – because of Windsor?

LATIMER: No, Windsor phoned after I'd spoken to you. I sent for you because I've seen Mrs Frobisher. She now admits she told me a pack

138

	of lies about her daughter, she's even prepared to go to the police about it.
KIMBER:	(*Apparently unperturbed*) Well, this is good news for you, Howard, if she's prepared to substantiate your story.
LATIMER:	Yes, but unfortunately she refuses to say why she lied.
KIMBER:	Is that so very important?
LATIMER:	It is to me. I want to know who's behind all this, who put her up to it.
KIMBER:	Well, I didn't, Howard, if that's what you're thinking.
LATIMER:	You sent her to see me.
KIMBER:	Only because the child puzzled me and I wanted a second opinion.

LATIMER is about to say something, hesitates, looks at KIMBER for a moment.

LATIMER:	George, who was Albert Kroner?
KIMBER:	(*After a pause*) He was a photographer, a Czech.
LATIMER:	Was he a friend of yours?
KIMBER:	No.
LATIMER:	You said you knew him.
KIMBER:	Yes, I knew him, but – he wasn't a friend of mine.
LATIMER:	Was he a patient?
KIMBER:	(*Hesitates*) Er – yes – in a manner of speaking.
LATIMER:	Why were the police interested in him?
KIMBER:	Were they?
LATIMER:	You know damn well they were!
KIMBER:	(*Looking at his watch*) Look, Howard, if you want to know anything about Kroner I should

	ask Windsor. He knows a great deal more about him than I do.
LATIMER:	All right, he's phoning me on Friday night. I'll ask him then.
KIMBER:	(*Looking at LATIMER; curious*) Why is he phoning you?

LATIMER doesn't reply. He looks at KIMBER and sits on the arm of the chair.

LATIMER:	George, are you a wealthy man?
KIMBER:	Good heavens, no!
LATIMER:	Windsor seems to think you are. He seems to think you've got four thousand pounds to throw away.
KIMBER:	Four thousand pounds?
LATIMER:	(*Nodding*) He asked me to deliver a message to you. He said: tell Kimber if he doesn't hand over four thousand pounds by Friday night I shall write a letter to Inspector Dane.
KIMBER:	(*Obviously worried*) A letter? What kind of a letter?
LATIMER:	Use your imagination. What kind of a letter would a man like Windsor write?
KIMBER:	(*Turning towards LATIMER*) Look, Howard, tell me – what did he say? What exactly did he say?
LATIMER:	I've told you what he said. He wants four thousand pounds.
KIMBER:	But he didn't say anything else? Didn't he tell you – what he was going to put in the letter?
LATIMER:	(*Shaking his head; watching KIMBER*) He said, just deliver the message. Kimber will understand. (*A moment*) Do you understand, George?

A pause.

KIMBER: (*Obviously worried*) Yes, I do. (*Dejected*) When do you say he's phoning – Friday?

LATIMER: (*Watching him*) Yes.

KIMBER: I don't know where the hell I'm going to get it from but I'll have the money here by Thursday morning. If he phones you before then tell him – it's all right.

LATIMER: George, did you murder Frieda Veldon?

KIMBER: I've told you I didn't!

LATIMER: Or Kroner?

KIMBER: I didn't murder either of them.

LATIMER: Then don't be a damn fool! Why should you give Windsor four thousand pounds just because he threatens to write a letter? Call his bluff, George!

KIMBER looks at LATIMER, hesitates on his way to the door.

KIMBER: I've underrated him once, Howard. I don't want to do it again.

CUT TO: *LAURA drives up to LATIMER's flat in Knightsbridge, in a taxi. She gets out of it and presses the bell push. She stands waiting for a reply but no one answers. After a moment she presses the bell again. There is still no reply; she looks at her watch. The door is thrown open by LATIMER who is holding a small hand towel.*

LATIMER: Sorry, Laura! I was in the bathroom. Come in!

CUT TO: LATIMER's living room.

LAURA enters followed by LATIMER. He crosses into the bedroom to dispose of the towel and then returns.

LATIMER: Would you like a drink?

LAURA: No, I don't think so, thank you, Howard.

LATIMER: Well, I think I'll have one.

LAURA:	(*Watching LATIMER*) You look tired.
LATIMER:	Yes, I am. I've had quite a day. (*Mixes himself a drink*) I'm so sorry I didn't speak to you on the phone this morning, Laura. I had Kimber with me.
LAURA:	What did he want?
LATIMER:	He didn't want anything. I asked him to call round and see me. (*Indicates decanter*) Are you sure you wouldn't like a drink?

LAURA senses that there is something the matter with LATIMER and that his casual friendliness is a cover.

LAURA:	Yes, I'm quite sure. Why did you send for Kimber?
LATIMER:	I wanted to have another talk with him. (*Drinks*) You don't like Kimber, do you, Laura? At least, you said you didn't.
LAURA:	I've only met him that once, I certainly didn't take to him on that occasion.

LATIMER sits on the arm of the chair.

LATIMER:	<u>Was</u> that the first time you'd met him?
LAURA:	(*Surprised by the question*) Why, yes, of course! You introduced us. (*Puzzled*) Did Kimber say we'd met before?
LATIMER:	No; I wondered, that's all. You seem to have met so many people, Laura. I thought perhaps you might have met Kimber.
LAURA:	Howard, you're annoyed about something. What is it?
LATIMER:	I'm not annoyed. I'm just disappointed, that's all.
LAURA:	Disappointed? What are you disappointed in?
LATIMER:	I'm disappointed in you, Laura. (*He puts down his drink; rises*) Why didn't you tell me at the beginning that you were mixed up in

142

	this business? Why didn't you tell me that you knew Geoffrey Windsor?
LAURA:	(*Puzzled*) Geoffrey Windsor? You mean that man that took you to the airport. The man that …
LATIMER:	You know perfectly well who I mean.
LAURA:	(*Suddenly angry*) I don't know who you mean! Look, Howard, you got yourself involved in this affair because you hadn't the common sense to put your cards on the table and be perfectly frank with everybody. And now you're making …
LATIMER:	That's not true! You know damn well it's not true!
LAURA:	It's perfectly true! And now you're making the same mistake all over again, only this time with me instead of Inspector Dane. Now if you've got anything to say, Howard, if there's anything at the back of your mind, please say it!

LATIMER looks at LAURA; hesitates, then:

LATIMER:	All right. This morning I had a phone call from Geoffrey Windsor. I met him at a coffee bar in Knightsbridge. He told me he intended to blackmail Kimber and that he wanted me to act as a go-between. Naturally, I refused.
LAURA:	Go on …
LATIMER:	When he realised I hadn't the slightest intention of doing what he wanted, he threatened to see Dane.
LAURA:	About Kimber?
LATIMER:	No – about you, Laura.
LAURA:	(*Surprised*) About me?
LATIMER:	Yes.

143

LAURA:	But I've never met him! He doesn't know anything about me!
LATIMER:	That wasn't my impression.
LAURA:	(*Suddenly; alarmed*) Howard, you didn't do what he wanted, did you? You didn't tell Kimber to …

LATIMER nods.

LAURA:	… But don't you realise if Kimber goes to the police they'll think it was you that was blackmailing him! They'll never believe your story.
LATIMER:	He won't go to the police.
LAURA:	What makes you so sure?
LATIMER:	(*Shaking his head*) He won't go to the police, Laura.
LAURA:	Well, supposing Dane learns about this from someone else?
LATIMER:	Who – for instance?
LAURA:	Well … Windsor.
LATIMER:	(*Puzzled*) Windsor?
LAURA:	Yes, supposing – after he gets what he wants – Windsor decides to double-cross you; supposing he tells the police that the whole idea was yours. That you blackmailed Kimber?
LATIMER:	He'd have to substantiate his story.
LAURA:	Would that be so very difficult, with a man like Kimber under his thumb? (*Shaking her head*) You shouldn't have seen Kimber, Howard. You shouldn't have told him what …
LATIMER:	(*Exasperated*) It's all very well telling me what I shouldn't have done – what should I have done, that's the point.

144

LAURA: You should have gone to the police yourself,
                straightaway.
LATIMER: (*A moment; quietly; watching her*) I can still
                do that, Laura.
LAURA: Then, why don't you?
LATIMER: I've told you why.
LAURA: Because of what Windsor said about me?
LATIMER: Yes.
A pause.
LAURA: There's only one answer to that, Howard.
*LAURA crosses to the table and picks up the telephone; she
dials a number. LATIMER stands watching her.*
LAURA: (*On phone*) Hello? ... I want to speak to
                Inspector Dane, please ... Thank you. (*A
                moment*) Inspector, this is Laura James ... My
                fiancé, Dr Latimer, has asked me to ring you.
                He'd like to see you ... Yes, as soon as
                possible. (*A moment*) Half-past six? ... Yes,
                that'll do nicely ... Thank you.
LAURA replaces the receiver.

CUT TO: *DETECTIVE INSPECTOR DANE is sitting behind
his desk in his office at New Scotland Yard. He picks up the
telephone and dials a number, smiling at LATIMER who is
sitting on the opposite side of the desk. DANE lifts the
receiver to his ear; casually trying to fill his pipe with his free
hand from a tobacco tin on the desk.*
DANE: (*On phone*) Put me through to Major
                Harrington, will you, please? (*A pause;
                DANE continues filling his pipe*) Hello –
                Major Harrington? This is Dane. I've got Dr
                Latimer with me at the moment ... Yes, he's
                in my office. (*Smiling*) I'd like him to meet
                you ... Well, we're going down to the

projection room, we should be back in about a quarter of an hour … Right – see you in my office.

DANE replaces the receiver and puts the lid on the tobacco tin.

DANE: (*Pressing the tobacco into his pipe*) That was Major Harrington; he's attached to our special branch. I think it's about time you met him, Dr Latimer.

LATIMER: (*Puzzled and faintly on edge*) Look, Inspector, I've told you what happened this morning. I've told you about Windsor and Kimber and my fiancée and you've made absolutely no comment whatsoever.

DANE: I didn't want to interrupt you, doctor.

LATIMER: You've interrupted me before – frequently.

DANE: Have I? Then, I apologise.

DANE looks at LATIMER; smiles; takes a match from the desk and lights his pipe.

LATIMER: You know, I can't make you out! I'm damned if I can make you out! I don't know whether you believe every word I tell you or you just don't believe anything.

DANE is faintly amused; fingers the bowl of his pipe.

DANE: Dr Latimer, during the past week, have you ever stopped and asked yourself why you haven't been arrested?

LATIMER: No.

DANE: You should have done.

LATIMER: I assumed you hadn't sufficient evidence.

DANE picks up a bulky file off the desk and tosses it towards LATIMER.

DANE: This is your dossier. There's enough evidence here to arrest you twenty times over.

146

LATIMER: Then why haven't you?

DANE smiles, rises, and comes from behind the desk. He puts a friendly hand on LATIMER's shoulder.

DANE: I'm a bird watcher, Dr Latimer. You're not the bird I'm after. (*Pats LATIMER's shoulder*) Come downstairs with me. I've got something to show you.

CUT TO: A Projection Room at New Scotland Yard. This is a long, narrow room, plainly furnished, and equipped with a 16 mm movie projector. The portable screen is at the far end of the room. The projector stands on a large table together with a tape-recording machine, a bio-scope, microscope, a box of slides, etc. There are several chairs in the room; a filing cabinet, a shortwave radio receiver.

A uniformed POLICEMAN (WILLIAMS) is sitting at a desk; he is showing DETECTIVE SERGEANT THOMAS a slide. We recognise THOMAS as the busker with   the   tambourine. The door opens and DR LATIMER enters with DANE. WILLIAMS rises from the desk.

DANE: Are you ready, Williams?

WILLIAMS: Yes, sir. Where shall we begin?

DANE: I think we'll have the recording first.

WILLIAMS nods and switches on the recorder. LATIMER is staring at THOMAS obviously puzzled.

DANE: Oh, this is Sergeant Thomas. Dr Latimer.

THOMAS: (*Shaking hands; smiling*) How do you do, sir? We've met before.

LATIMER: (*Staring at THOMAS puzzled*) Yes, I realise that, but I can't remember where.

DANE: (*Smiling*) You will. (*To LATIMER*) Sit down, doctor. (*Indicates the recorder*) I want you to listen to this.

147

LATIMER sits in one of the chairs, he stares across at WILLIAMS, obviously bewildered. WILLIAMS starts the machine. From the recording machine we hear LATIMER's voice; it is obviously a recording of a telephone conversation.

LATIMER: Hello?

MAN's VOICE: Is that you Howard?

LATIMER: Who is that?

MAN's VOICE: (*Impatiently; yet in a good humour*) Who the devil do you think it is? It's Charles.

LATIMER: (*Astonished*) Charles!

MAN: Yes, Charles, old boy. Charles Kaufmann. Look, Howard, I've been trying to get in touch with you all day ...

LATIMER: (*Tensely; interrupting him*) Charles, where are you? Where are you speaking from?

As LATIMER speaks there is the sound of a thud and the noise of the receiver falling out of his hand.

MAN: Hello? ... What's happened ... Howard ... Howard, can you hear me? ... Hello? Hello? Hello, there!

The noise of the receiver being replaced. WILLIAMS switches off the recorder.

DANE: Do you recognise it?

LATIMER rises.

LATIMER: Why, yes of course! That's Charles – that's our phone conversation when I was knocked on the head.

DANE: That's right.

LATIMER: (*Incredulously*) Have you been listening to all my telephone calls?

DANE: Only the interesting ones. Sit down, doctor. We haven't finished yet.

DANE nods to WILLIAMS, who crosses, switches out the light and returns to the movie projector.

148

DANE: (*To LATIMER*) I want you to watch this film.
             (*To WILLIAMS*) Right, Williams.

WILLIAMS switches on the projector and the film is projected onto the screen at the far end of the room.

CUT TO: FILM SEQUENCE: *This short film excerpt shows the troupe of buskers outside of the coffee bar in Knightsbridge. DETECTIVE SERGEANT THOMAS is easily recognised. The film is shot as if the camera is concealed in the hurdy-gurdy. Numerous people pass in and out of the coffee bar. WINDSOR suddenly appears on the scene, walking towards the coffee bar from the other side of the road.*

LATIMER: That's Windsor!

DANE: Yes, I know. Wait a minute!

As WINDSOR reaches the coffee bar a man comes out and obviously says something to him. WINDSOR nods and goes into the coffee bar. The camera follows the stranger across the pavement. THOMAS crosses to the man and stops him. The man feels in his pocket, drops a coin into the tambourine, then walks away.

DANE: Do you know that man?

LATIMER: No, I've never seen him before.

DANE: Are you sure, doctor?

LATIMER: Yes, I'm quite sure.

A taxi drives up to the kerb and LATIMER gets out. He turns to pay the driver. THOMAS walks across to LATIMER and holds out his tambourine.

DANE: (*Satisfied*) Thank you, Williams.

WILLIAMS stops the film and THOMAS crosses and switches on the light.

THOMAS: (*To LATIMER: smiling*) Now you know where we met, doctor.

149

LATIMER:	Yes, but – (*Turns to DANE; confused*) Look, Inspector, don't you think you owe me an explanation?
DANE:	(*Smiling*) Yes, I do. But I'd like you to meet Major Harrington first. He's got quite a lot to tell you.
LATIMER:	Major Harrington?
DANE:	(*Nodding*) Yes, he's been in charge of this affair from the very beginning.

DANE crosses and opens the door.

| DANE: | Come along, doctor. |

LATIMER moves towards the door, hesitates, then turns and looks at THOMAS. The SERGEANT grins.

| LATIMER: | (*Suddenly; smiling*) I think you owe me sixpence. |

CUT TO: DETECTIVE INSPECTOR DANE's office.

A man is sitting in a wing chair smoking a cigar; we cannot see the man himself, only the hand holding the cigar resting on the arm of the chair. The door opens and DANE enters followed by LATIMER. LATIMER moves into the room and then suddenly stops, a look of complete astonishment on his face. The man gets out of the chair and smiles at LATIMER. It is ROBERT BRADY.

| DANE: | This is the gentleman I was telling you about, doctor. Major Harrington. |

LATIMER stares across at BRADY, alias HARRINGTON.

END OF EPISODE FIVE

EPISODE SIX

OPEN TO: DETECTIVE INSPECTOR DANE's Office.

The door opens and DANE enters, followed by LATIMER. LATIMER moves into the room and stops in astonishment as he sees ROBERT BRADY is there.

DANE: This is the gentleman I was telling you about, doctor. Major Harrington.

BRADY: Good evening, Dr Latimer.

BRADY rises.

LATIMER: (*To DANE; tensely*) But this is Brady! This is the man that came to Ken Palmer's – the man that wanted the matches!

DANE: (*Quietly; smiling*) Yes, I know.

BRADY: (*Indicating a chair*) I think we owe you an explanation.

LATIMER: Well, someone certainly does!

BRADY: (*To DANE*) Shall I begin, Inspector?

DANE: (*Nodding*) Yes; but before you begin I think there's something we ought to tell Dr Latimer. (*To LATIMER*) We knew you didn't murder Frieda Veldon, sir, and we realise you had nothing to do with the Kroner affair.

LATIMER: (*Relieved; yet puzzled*) You mean, you don't suspect me?

DANE: We never have done, sir, not seriously.

LATIMER: Well, why in heaven's name didn't you tell me that?

DANE: We couldn't, doctor.

LATIMER: Why not?

BRADY: (*Smiling*) We just couldn't, Dr Latimer.

LATIMER sits.

LATIMER: Look, forgive me – but who the devil are you exactly?

BRADY: My name is Harrington. Brady Harrington. I'm attached to Scotland Yard but for the past

153

two years I've been working with Interpol. (*Smiling*) I expect you've heard of it?

LATIMER: That's the International Police Organisation?

BRADY: Yes, that's right. Well, two years ago I was sent out to Germany to investigate a group called Die Grenze. That's a German word meaning a frontier or boundary. They specialised in supplying forged passports, illegal permits, visas, that sort of thing.

LATIMER: (*Interested*) Go on.

BRADY: Well, I discovered that if you wanted to get in touch with the organisation you had to visit a certain café in Berlin. The café was called 'Der Bronzone Kerzonhalter'.

LATIMER: The brass candlestick?

BRADY: (*Nodding*) Once the proprietor of the café was satisfied that you were genuine he passed you on to a man called Albert Kroner.

DANE: Kroner was in direct touch with a man known in the organisation as Henson, and it's this man that we're chiefly interested in.

LATIMER: Why's that?

DANE: We believe Henson operates in England and virtually controls the whole set-up.

LATIMER: But how did Frieda Veldon fit into all this?

BRADY: Miss Veldon was wanted by the West German police for larceny and Die Grenze supplied her with a false passport. It was intended that she should contact Henson in London, pick up an American visa, and travel through to New York. Unfortunately for Miss Veldon it didn't work out that way.

LATIMER: But why didn't it – she got to London all right?

154

BRADY: Yes, but information had already reached Henson that several of his colleagues had been arrested. He realised that we might be on to him next and that his best bet was to divert suspicion onto someone else. Unfortunately, he picked on you, Dr Latimer.

DANE: He knew that you were friendly with Charles Kaufmann, so he impersonated Kaufmann and asked you to meet Miss Veldon at London Airport. Later he murdered her and planted the murder weapon – the brass candlestick – in your car.

LATIMER: But why pick on a brass candlestick?

DANE: He picked on it for two reasons. One: because he thought it would give us the impression that you were connected with Die Grenze. Two: because he'd already blackmailed Mrs Frobisher into telling you a story about a candlestick.

LATIMER: Well – how did that help him?

DANE: He knew you'd tell us about Mrs Frobisher. He felt sure that when her story wasn't substantiated, we'd be more convinced than ever that you were lying – that you were in fact the murderer.

BRADY: Henson left nothing to chance. You remember the afternoon you picked up Miss James's shoes?

LATIMER: I do indeed!

BRADY: When you called into the hospital again on the way home Kimber switched the parcels. In the meantime, someone – presumably Henson – telephoned the Yard and told the Inspector that you were concealing part of the

	murder weapon. In order to examine the parcel – and not divulge my identity – I'm afraid I had to be slightly melodramatic.
DANE:	(*Smiling*) We don't always approve of Major Harrington's methods, Dr Latimer.
BRADY:	You don't always know about them, Bill.
DANE:	That's absolutely true!
LATIMER:	But what happened that afternoon – I thought you'd been shot?
BRADY:	It was a blank cartridge, but it gave me a nasty burn. (*Amused*) I was so surprised I forgot the parcel!
DANE:	I might add, Dr Latimer, he got very little sympathy in this quarter!
LATIMER:	But tell me about Windsor: were you watching him?
BRADY:	Yes. I actually followed you out to the Airport. Besides being a professional blackmailer, Windsor's an associate of Henson's. We were hoping Windsor would lead us to him.
LATIMER:	I see. But tell me: why did Miss Veldon give me the book of matches?
BRADY:	She thought you represented Henson and she gave you the matches to prove her identity; apparently the book of matches was always used for that purpose.
LATIMER:	But you wanted them, you asked me to get them for you.
BRADY:	Yes, because I thought they might contain a secret message which would lead us to Henson.
DANE:	You'll gather that Henson is the bird we're after, Dr Latimer.

LATIMER: So, Windsor was working for Henson – did he know that I was going to get that phone call?

DANE: Of course he did; that's why he was in your consulting room and why he put Frieda Veldon's name in your appointment book.

BRADY: And, Henson, I suppose, put the appointment in the diary.

LATIMER: I see. (*Thoughtfully*) But tell me – what has my friend Charles, Charles Kaufmann – got to do with all this?

DANE: (*Shaking his head*) So far as we know he's still in New York; he was certainly there twenty-four hours ago.

LATIMER: Well – why did Henson keep on phoning me and pretending he was Charles? I can see the point of the first phone call but why the subsequent ones?

BRADY: He knew we'd check on Kaufmann and find he couldn't possibly have made any of the calls, and that would make you look a bigger liar than ever.

LATIMER: Well, this Mr Henson certainly seems to have had it in for me!

BRADY: He does indeed. That's why … We thought you might like to help us.

LATIMER: (*Puzzled*) How can I help you?

BRADY: I'll tell you how, Dr Latimer.

CUT TO: DR LATIMER's Consulting Room.
NURSE KAY enters with a pile of letters and crosses to the desk where she arranges the letters. LATIMER enters.

LATIMER: Good morning, Nurse.

KAY: (*Turning*) Oh, good morning, doctor!

LATIMER:	You got my message?
KAY:	Yes, sir.
LATIMER:	Well – what's happened?
KAY:	Mrs Harris was the difficulty, however, I've made an appointment for six o'clock tomorrow evening.
LATIMER:	Good. So I've got no appointments this morning?
KAY:	No, sir – they've all been cancelled, except Dr Kimber.
LATIMER:	(*Smiling*) Thank you, Nurse.
KAY:	(*Puzzled*) Aren't you feeling very well, doctor?
LATIMER:	Yes, I'm feeling fine – why?
KAY:	Well, I just wondered why you'd cancelled all your appointments.
LATIMER:	Oh. Oh, I see. Any messages?
KAY:	Yes, Miss James telephoned about half-an-hour ago.
LATIMER:	What did she say?
KAY:	She said she'd telephoned your flat and couldn't get any reply. She's phoning again later.
LATIMER:	I don't want to talk to my fiancée this morning, Nurse. When she phones tell her I've been detained at the hospital.
KAY:	(*Quietly; baffled*) Very well, doctor.
LATIMER:	I'll see Dr Kimber the moment he arrives.
KAY:	Yes, sir.

NURSE KAY exits and shuts the door.

CUT TO: As before.
The door opens and GEORGE KIMBER enters carrying a brief case.

LATIMER:	Hello, George. Sit down.
KIMBER:	No, thank you.
LATIMER:	(*Pleasantly*) What is it you want to see me about?
KIMBER:	(*Surprised*) What is it I want to see you about?
LATIMER:	Yes.
KIMBER:	(*Astonished*) Why – Why it's Friday!
LATIMER:	Yes, I know it's Friday. (*Looking at the calendar on his desk*) Friday, March 16th.
KIMBER:	Howard, have you forgotten – have you forgotten about Windsor?
LATIMER:	(*Suddenly*) Good Lord, of course! Windsor! I'm sorry, George. I've had other things to think about.
KIMBER:	(*Irritated by LATIMER's attitude*) Well, you're damn lucky! I wish I'd had other things to think about. I take it you haven't heard from him?
LATIMER:	No, not yet, George. (*Smiling*) But I will. What do you want me to do when I hear from him?
KIMBER:	(*After a moment's pause; indicating the case*) You can give him this.
LATIMER:	You've got the money?
KIMBER:	Yes.
LATIMER:	Four thousand pounds?
KIMBER:	(*Irritated*) Yes.
LATIMER:	Congratulations. It isn't everyone that can raise four thousand pounds at a moment's notice.

KIMBER: Howard, I've had the devil of a time getting this money. I want to make quite sure that … (*Hesitates*)

LATIMER: Quite sure of what, George?

KIMBER: (*Obviously worried*) Look, I know I've asked you this before, but what exactly did Windsor say to you?

LATIMER: I've told you what he said: he said he wanted four thousand pounds and if you didn't give it to him, he'd write to Inspector Dane.

KIMBER: He didn't say what he'd write to Dane about?

LATIMER: No, but presumably you know that, otherwise you wouldn't be so keen on handing him the four thousand.

KIMBER: Howard, if Windsor knows what I think he knows, he can ruin me – on the other hand if he's bluffing …

LATIMER: Well, you can easily find out if he's bluffing.

KIMBER: How?

LATIMER: (*Rising from the desk*) Call his bluff. Tell him to write to Dane; tell him to write to the whole of Scotland Yard if he feels like it.

KIMBER: That isn't quite so easy as it sounds. (*He looks at LATIMER for a moment*) What would you do, Howard – if you were in my shoes?

LATIMER: I know what I should do. I should go to the Yard and tell them the whole story.

KIMBER: (*Quietly*) I wonder.

LATIMER: George, supposing you give Windsor this money, do you think that's going to satisfy him?

KIMBER: It's got to satisfy him! I've raised every penny I could lay my hands on!

NURSE KAY enters.

LATIMER: (*Shaking his head*) I'll bet you anything you like that within six months he'll … (*Breaks off on seeing the NURSE*)

KAY: Excuse me, sir, but Inspector Dane would like to see you. I told him you were engaged, but …

DANE enters accompanied by a plain clothed SERGEANT.

DANE: (*Dismissing the NURSE*) That's all right, Nurse – thank you.

NURSE KAY exits.

LATIMER: (*Apparently angry*) What is it, Inspector? You can see I'm busy!

DANE: (*With authority*) Dr Latimer, I want you to come down to the station with me.

LATIMER: (*Indignantly*) Why?

DANE: I'll tell you why when we get to the station.

LATIMER: Are you arresting me, Inspector?

DANE: (*Bluntly*) I'm asking you to come down to the station, sir.

LATIMER: Now?

DANE: Yes, now, doctor. Straight away.

LATIMER: But this is absurd, absolutely absurd! I've several patients coming to see me this morning …

DANE: Then I suggest you put them off.

LATIMER: Don't be ridiculous, man! How can I put them off?

DANE: That's your problem, doctor.

DANE nods to the SERGEANT.

DANE: (*Quietly*) Are you ready, Dr Latimer?

LATIMER: (*Apparently perturbed; to KIMBER*) I'll see you this afternoon, George – at the flat.

KIMBER: (*Nodding*) Yes, all right, Howard.

LATIMER goes out, followed by the Plain Clothes man. DANE looks at KIMBER then turns towards the door.

161

CUT TO: Front page of a newspaper featuring a story that the police are about to arrest LATIMER

CUT TO: LATIMER's Flat.
The phone rings and LATIMER answers it.
LATIMER: (*On phone*) Hello?

CUT TO: Telephone Box.
GEOFFREY WINDSOR is in it with the receiver to his ear. He presses button "A"
WINDSOR: Hello? Is that Dr Latimer?
LATIMER: Yes, who is that?
WINDSOR: This is Geoffrey Windsor.
LATIMER: Oh – hello, Windsor.
WINDSOR: Well, what's happened? Have you seen Kimber?
LATIMER: Yes, I've seen him, and he's got the money. It'll be here for you.
WINDSOR: Good! (*Pleased*) Now, I'll tell you what I want you to do.

CUT TO: LATIMER's Flat. As before.
LATIMER: (*Suddenly; taking the initiative*) You're not telling me anything, Windsor. The money'll be here. If you want it, come and get it. (*He replaces the receiver, before WINDSOR can reply*)
LATIMER plants a microphone. The doorbell rings. LATIMER goes into the hall and opens the door to find LAURA there. She is holding a newspaper.
LATIMER: Laura!
LAURA: Howard, what's happened? I've been trying to get in touch with you all day!

LAURA enters and goes through to the lounge. HOWARD closes the door and follows LAURA.

LAURA: Why are you avoiding me? I've been to
             Harley Street twice, I've even been to the
             Hospital …

LATIMER: Laura, listen to me! A great deal's happened
             since I saw you last.

LAURA: Yes, I know. I've seen the papers. (*Showing
             him the newspaper*) Howard, are they really
             going to arrest you?

LATIMER: (*Shaking his head*) No, no, Laura …

LAURA: But it says here that they took you down to
             the station. It says the Inspector …

LATIMER: (*Quickly; tensely*) Yes, I know what it says,
             darling. I've read it. (*Holding her*) Look,
             Laura, I want you to do something for me.
             Go back to your flat and wait – wait until I
             phone you – when I phone, I'll explain
             everything.

LAURA: (*Alarmed*) Howard, are you running away?
             Because if you are …

LATIMER: No, no, I'm not running away, honestly,
             darling. I'll explain everything later.

LAURA: (*A shade angry*) Why can't you explain now?
             I've a right to know what's happened, you
             can't just leave me in the dark like this!

LATIMER: (*Tensely*) Look, Laura, please! I can't tell
             you now. I've given my word that I won't say
             …

The doorbell rings.

LATIMER: (*A shade tense*) That's Kimber. I'm expecting
             him. Please do as I tell you. Please, Laura.

LAURA: All right, Howard.

163

They walk out into the hall. LATIMER opens the front door and KIMBER enters.

LATIMER: Oh, hello, George!
KIMBER: Oh!
LATIMER: I think you've met Laura.
KIMBER: Yes, I have. Good afternoon, Miss James.
LAURA: Good afternoon.
LATIMER: (*To LAURA*) I'll phone you later, darling.
LAURA: (*After a moment*) Yes, all right. Don't forget, Howard. I shall be waiting …

LAURA leaves and LATIMER closes the door. He and KIMBER move through to the living room.

KIMBER: Have you heard from Windsor?
LATIMER: Yes, I've heard. He phoned me about five minutes ago. (*Crosses to the drinks table, and commences to mix himself a drink*) George, I'm in a spot. One hell of a spot.
KIMBER: Yes, I know. What happened this morning?
LATIMER: (*Looking up; tensely*) I'll tell you what happened. They took me down to the station and questioned me for three hours. Three hours, George! My God, I thought they'd never stop!
KIMBER: (*Nervously*) You didn't tell them about me and …
LATIMER: (*Turning on him; angry*) I didn't tell them anything! What's the point? They don't believe me, anyhow – they don't believe a word I say! (*He drinks*) It's my bet by this time tomorrow, they'll have a warrant out for me. (*Looks at KIMBER; points to case*) George, I'm doing you a favour over this Windsor business. Now, you can do me one!
KIMBER: (*Apprehensive*) What is it?

LATIMER: The police think I murdered Kroner. I didn't. You know darn well I didn't.

KIMBER: Well?

LATIMER: Who did murder him?

KIMBER: (*After a moment; obviously worried*) Kroner was a member of an organisation called Die Grenze; he came here because things were getting too hot on the Continent. The whole set-up's controlled by an Englishman – a man called Henson. (*He turns away*) It was Henson that murdered Kroner.

LATIMER: Are you a member of this organisation?

KIMBER: (*Turning back*) No. No, I'm not. About a year ago, I had an affair with a girl called – well, I suddenly learnt that she was mixed up in a murder case. Although it had nothing to do with me, she threatened to drag me into it. She introduced me to Henson; he offered to get her out of the country in return for …

LATIMER: In return for what?

KIMBER: He wanted a supply of heroin. I got it for him.

LATIMER: (*Angry*) Why, you damn fool!

KIMBER: (*A shrug*) Whether the whole thing was a put up job or not, I don't know. One way or another, they've been blackmailing me ever since.

KIMBER looks out of the window.

LATIMER: And Mrs Frobisher? Have they been blackmailing her?

KIMBER: Yes. Yes, they have. I don't know what hold they've got over her, but … (*He stops; obviously sees someone through the window*) Here's Windsor – he's just arrived! Howard, I don't want to see him!

165

LATIMER: All right. You can go out the back way.
They go out.

CUT TO: The street outside of LATIMER's flat.
GEOFFREY WINDSOR gets out of his car.

CUT TO: LATIMER's flat. As before.
WINDSOR enters followed by LATIMER.
WINDSOR: You sounded very sure of yourself on the telephone, Doctor. Having seen the papers, I can't imagine why.
LATIMER: (*Pointing to the case*) There's the money – take it and get out.
WINDSOR: Delighted.
WINDSOR opens the case, looks inside and closes it again.
LATIMER: Aren't you going to count it?
WINDSOR: Eventually.
WINDSOR picks up the case and starts to walk to the alcove.
LATIMER: (*Suddenly; obviously tense*) Windsor, wait a minute.
WINDSOR: Well?
LATIMER looks at WINDSOR; hesitates
WINDSOR: Well – what is it?
LATIMER: I want to talk to you. There's something I want to ask you.
WINDSOR: (*Turning away*) I'm not in a talkative mood.
LATIMER: No, Windsor – wait! You've got four thousand pounds in that case.
WINDSOR: Well?
LATIMER: How would you like to double it?
WINDSOR: (*After a moment*) Do you know how I can double it, Dr Latimer?
LATIMER: Yes, I do.
WINDSOR: How?

LATIMER:	(*After a pause; turning towards the drinks on the table*) Have a drink, Windsor.
WINDSOR:	I don't want a drink.
LATIMER:	Well, do you mind if I have one?
WINDSOR:	(*Impatiently*) Look, if you've got a proposition, Latimer – let's have it.
LATIMER:	(*Turning; holding a glass*) You've seen the papers, you know what a serious position I'm in. It's probably only a matter of hours before they pick me up.
WINDSOR:	That's no concern of mine.
LATIMER:	(*Suddenly; tense*) Yes, it is! You know who murdered Frieda Veldon! You could go to the police and tell them the whole story.
WINDSOR:	(*Interrupting him*) Is that your proposition?
LATIMER:	I'll give you six thousand pounds if you go to Dane and tell him …
WINDSOR:	(*With almost contempt*) I wouldn't go to Dane if you offered me six million! Do you think I was born yesterday? (*Moves towards alcove*) You're in a jam, doctor – and you're going to stay that way!
LATIMER:	Am I Windsor? We shall see. I've been pushed around long enough, my friend. Now I'm taking the initiative for a change.
WINDSOR:	What do you mean?
LATIMER:	I'm getting out. I'm leaving the country.
WINDSOR:	(*Shaking his head*) Don't be a damn fool! Once they've issued a warrant, you've had it. You won't get further than Hammersmith.
LATIMER:	We shall see,
WINDSOR:	(*Quietly*) You said just now, you'd give me six thousand pounds if I talked to Dane.
LATIMER:	(*Turning*) Yes.

167

WINDSOR: Supposing that instead of talking to Dane I were to help you some other way.

LATIMER: What other way?

WINDSOR: Would you still pay the six thousand?

LATIMER: It depends …

WINDSOR: On what?

LATIMER: (*Watching WINDSOR*) On what you did.

WINDSOR sits on the arm of a chair.

WINDSOR: Are you serious about making a dash for it, about leaving the country?

LATIMER: Of course I'm serious! Good God, what would you do if you were in my shoes?

WINDSOR: Supposing I said I know someone who could smuggle you out – right under the nose of Dane and the whole of Scotland Yard, if necessary.

LATIMER: I should be impressed by your imagination, Mr Windsor – that's all.

WINDSOR: I'm serious, doctor.

LATIMER: Then where's the snag?

WINDSOR: (*Quietly looks up at LATIMER; shaking his head*) There isn't one.

LATIMER: (*Tensely*) Well – what happens? What do I do? There isn't a lot of time!

WINDSOR: I've got to contact a man called Henson; if he's interested he'll take over.

LATIMER: And supposing he isn't interested?

WINDSOR: (*Smiling*) Somehow, I think he will.

WINDSOR rises

LATIMER: Because of the money?

WINDSOR: Partly – and partly because he's got a sense of humour. I think he'd find the situation to his liking, Dr Latimer.

LATIMER: Who is this man – Henson? I've never heard of him.

WINDSOR: He's head of an organisation called Die Grenze.

LATIMER: Die Grenze?

WINDSOR: Yes. Don't worry, you'll be in very good hands.

LATIMER: You mean, he's done this before – smuggled people out of the country?

WINDSOR: (*Smiling*) In and out, Dr Latimer. In and out. (*Points to the telephone*) Is this the only phone you've got?

LATIMER: No, there's an extension in the bedroom.

WINDSOR: (*Nodding*) I'll use that.

WINDSOR heads toward the bedroom; then turns.

WINDSOR: I'm not suggesting that you would, but I advise you not to listen, Dr Latimer.

WINDSOR goes into the bedroom and closes the door. LATIMER watches. He hears the phone tinkle. He paces the room; anxious. After a while WINDSOR returns.

LATIMER: Well – what did he say?

A pause.

WINDSOR: He wants to see you. I'm meeting him here at four o'clock. Don't go out and don't answer the door. I shan't use the bell, I'll knock.

LATIMER: (*Quietly*) All right.

WINDSOR goes out to the hall and opens the front door and goes out.

CUT TO: LATIMER's flat. As before.

LATIMER is in the hall with the door open. KEN PALMER enters carrying a golf putter.

PALMER: I thought you were dead, Howard! I've been tolling the jolly old bell for all it's worth!

LATIMER: I think it's out of order.

PALMER: (*Indicating the putter*) I've brought the magic wand back. Wasn't any good, old man. Didn't work.

LATIMER: I didn't guarantee it.

PALMER: Good job, old boy. I should have demanded my money back.

They go through to the living room.

PALMER: Howard, why aren't you at Harley Street or at the hospital or somewhere?

LATIMER: I'm doing another article for The Lancet. I can write better at home.

PALMER: (*Laughing*) Come off it! They've found you out, Squire, that's what it is. They've analysed the old tonic and discovered it was sherbet with a dash of H.2.O.

LATIMER: (*Smiling*) I was just having some tea, Ken. Would you like some?

PALMER: Tea? I'd like a whisky and soda.

LATIMER: At four o'clock in the afternoon.

PALMER: Have you ever had a whisky and soda at four o'clock in the afternoon?

LATIMER: No, I can't say I have.

PALMER: (*Laughing*) Well, you don't know what you've been missing!

LATIMER: (*Quietly*) Have you seen the papers, Ken?

PALMER: The papers?

LATIMER: Yes.

PALMER: (*Mixing drinks*) No, I haven't. I've been out at Sunningdale all day. I was on the first tee at nine o'clock. (*Offers LATIMER a glass*) Here we are, old boy.

LATIMER: (*Taking glass*) Thanks.

PALMER: (*Turning from table*) Why – what's in the papers?

LATIMER: The police picked me up this morning. They questioned me for nearly three hours.

PALMER: I say, that couldn't have been very pleasant.

LATIMER: It wasn't.

PALMER: Three hours? Ye Gods, that's quite a session. What were they on about? Kroner, I suppose. (*Looks at his glass*) That fellow Dane can ask some pretty footling questions, can't he?

LATIMER: He can and he did. (*Quietly; watching PALMER*) You've had quite a few drinks, haven't you?

PALMER: (*Smiling*) Had one or two, old boy. Lost the match, had to drown my sorrows. You know how it is. (*Raises his glass*) Skoal. (*Empties the glass*)

LATIMER puts his drink down on table.

LATIMER: If you don't mind, I won't have this, not at the moment.

PALMER: All right, Howard. (*Smiles*) Please yourself.

A moment.

LATIMER: Ken, don't think me rude but I've got rather a lot to do this afternoon.

PALMER: Oh. (*Looks at his glass; suddenly*) Oh, well, I'll just have one for the road and then I'll be off.

The doorbell rings.

PALMER: Are you expecting someone, Howard?

LATIMER: Yes, I am as a matter of fact.

PALMER: Oh. (*A sudden thought*) Oh, I get it! (*Grins*) I gather I've dropped in at an awkward moment.

171

LATIMER:	You have, but not for the reason you're thinking.
PALMER:	Come off it! (*Moves towards LATIMER*) Who is she? Do I know her?
LATIMER:	(*Irritated*) Look, Ken, it's nothing like that. I'm expecting someone on business – very important business. (*Looks at his watch*) I'd be awfully grateful if you'd go.
PALMER:	Well, I will, Howard. Just say the word.
LATIMER:	Ken, I've said the word! I want you to go!
PALMER:	You're waiting for Windsor, aren't you?
LATIMER:	(*Apparently surprised*) Yes. Yes – how did you know?
PALMER:	There's no need to wait for him. We can dispense with Mr Windsor's services on this occasion.
LATIMER:	What do you mean?
PALMER:	(*A moment; looking at the putter*) Windsor telephoned me about an hour ago.
LATIMER:	Telephoned <u>you</u>?
PALMER:	Yes.
LATIMER:	I thought you said you were at Sunningdale, playing golf.
PALMER:	I was, this morning – (*Smiling*) Only this morning, fortunately.
LATIMER:	Ken, I don't understand this …
PALMER:	Don't you? (*Faces LATIMER*) It's not difficult to understand, Howard. I'm the person you're really waiting for. I'm Henson.
LATIMER:	(*Quietly; apparently astonished*) Henson?
PALMER:	Yes.
LATIMER:	Then you murdered Frieda Veldon! (*Pause*) And Kroner?
PALMER:	Yes – and Kroner.

LATIMER: (*Tensely; angry*) Then it was you that got me into all this – it was you that impersonated Charles?

PALMER: Yes, of course. (*Strolls across the room holding the putter; finally stops in front of the corner cupboard*) I was on the stage for two years, you know that. Besides, who else knew about your association with Charles Kaufmann? Only Kimber – and Kimber hasn't got the imagination of a mouse.

LATIMER: (*Controlling his anger*) But why did you do it? Why did you pick on me?

PALMER: I had to pick on somebody, old boy. I had to have a scapegoat. Besides, I wasn't feeling very friendly towards you, after what happened with Laura.

LATIMER: (*Puzzled*) Laura?

PALMER: Yes. I made a pass at her. Didn't she tell you? (*Looks at putter*) She gave me the brush-off. Wasn't very pleasant. Wasn't at all pleasant. Made me bloody angry as a matter of fact. (*Looks at LATIMER*) Well, I got you into this mess, now I'll get you out of it. (*Amused*) That's fair, isn't it?

LATIMER: (*Quietly*) Windsor said it would appeal to your sense of humour.

PALMER: He was right. (*Taps his wallet pocket*) Also my pocket, old boy. Six thousand isn't to be sneezed at. (*Looks at the putter, then at the cupboard. Quite casual*) Where does this go – in here?

LATIMER: (*A shade too quickly*) No! No, I've taken my clubs down to … (*He stops*)

173

PALMER looks at LATIMER, then at the cupboard. He jumps forward and throws open the cupboard door and sees a working tape recorder in the cupboard.

PALMER: What the hell's this? What does this mean?

PALMER moves swiftly to the window. He looks out and sees police standing by a police car.

PALMER: You knew! You knew I was Henson!

LATIMER: (*Quietly; facing PALMER*) Yes. I've suspected you for some time. You remember the day you came back from Wimbledon? You said you'd cut your hand? (S*haking his head*) That was an excuse to go into the bathroom – you were looking for a note that Mrs Frobisher sent me.

PALMER takes a knife out of his pocket.

LATIMER: (*Watching PALMER's hand*) Don't be a damn fool! Put that thing down!

PALMER is about to throw the knife at LATIMER. They begin to tussle when the police ((including DANE and BRADY) burst through the door. The police grab PALMER from behind and the knife drops to the floor. PALMER also falls to the floor. The police pick him up and PALMER is taken out.

DANE: Are you all right, doctor?

LATIMER: Yes, I think so. But I'm not quite so fit as I thought I was!

BRADY: (*Smiling*) You did extremely well, sir. We're very grateful.

LATIMER: I hope you'll tell the press that, Major Harrington. (*Points to the newspaper on the settee*) I could do with some good publicity for a change!

DANE: Don't worry, we'll see you get it, sir!

BRADY: (*Nodding*) They'll have the full story in an hour.

BRADY goes out

POLICE OFFICER: (*To DANE*) The recorder, sir?

DANE: (*Nodding towards the cupboard*) It's in the cupboard. Just take the tape, we'll pick the machine up later.

LAURA enters.

LATIMER: (*Surprised*) Laura! (*Crosses to her*) Darling, what are you doing here?

DANE: Miss James has been sitting in my car for the last ten minutes. (*Smiling*) I think she thought we were going to arrest you, sir.

LATIMER: Does that surprise you, Inspector?

LAURA: (*To LATIMER*) I knew something was happening this afternoon, Howard. I just couldn't keep away!

DANE: I'll say good-bye sir.

LATIMER: (*Shaking hands*) Good-bye, Inspector.

DANE: If there's anything else I can do for you, just let me know.

LATIMER: (*Nodding*) Whenever I'm in need of a snappy third degree I'll give you a ring, Inspector.

DANE: Oh, we haven't treated you all that badly, sir!

DANE goes out, followed by the police officer with the tape. LAURA turns to LATIMER.

LAURA: Howard, are you all right?

LATIMER: (*Taking hold of her arm*) Yes. I'm sorry I thought you were mixed up in this, darling. I ought to have realised Windsor was lying.

LAURA smiles.

LATIMER: But, Laura – why didn't you tell me about Ken Palmer?

LAURA: What do you mean?

LATIMER: Why didn't you tell me he made a pass at you?

175

LAURA: Oh, lots of men make passes at me. You did.
LATIMER: (*A shade indignant*) I did?!
LAURA: Yes.
LATIMER: When?
LAURA: At Monte Carlo.
LATIMER: (*Dismissing it*) Oh, that was years ago.
LAURA: Was it?
LATIMER: Good heavens, yes! We've been engaged three years.
LAURA: I'm glad you mentioned it, Dr Latimer.

The telephone rings. LATIMER picks up the receiver.

LATIMER: (*On phone*) Hello?
CHARLES: (*On other end*) Howard – is that you?
LATIMER: Who is that?
CHARLES: (*Full of himself*) What d'you mean – who is it? It's Charles!
LATIMER: (*Staggered*) Charles!
CHARLES: Yes, Charles! Charles Kaufmann!
LATIMER: (*Stunned*) Where are you, Charles? Where are you speaking from?
CHARLES: I'm at the Airport. I've just flown in from New York. Look, Howard, why not come down here to-night and have dinner with me? I'm leaving for Paris at nine o'clock.
LATIMER: No … No, I'm sorry, Charles. I'm terribly sorry, but –
CHARLES: (*Laughing*) What d'you mean, you're terribly sorry?
LATIMER: I'm – I'm terribly sorry, Charles, I just can't make it.
CHARLES: Don't give me that, you old Sawbones. You jump in that car of yours and get down here!

LATIMER puts the receiver down on the table and the camera focusses on it with the voice of CHARLES at the other end.

176

CHARLES: Howard, did you hear me? ... Are you listening? ... Gee, what's happened to this tin-pot outfit? ... Howard, are you there? ... If you can hear me for goodness sake say something! ... Howard, I want to see you. I want you to have dinner with me ... I – Can you hear me? ... Howard, this is Charles!!!

THE END

Press Pack

Press cuttings about *My Friend Charles* ...

Stand By For A New Chiller by Max North

Keep your Saturday nights free in March and April. That master of suspense Francis Durbridge has written a new thriller serial called *My Friend Charles*.

And if it is up to the standard of the nerve-quivering *Portrait of Alison*, I, for one, shall be chained to my set.

Durbridge behaved mysteriously, rather like one of his fictional suspicious characters, when I phoned him this week at his home in Walton-on-Thames.

The phone was answered by a low, quick voice. "Yes?" it asked tensely.

"Is Mr Durbridge there?"

Pause for rapid calculation. "Who's calling?"

"Max North, *Manchester Evening News*."

"Oh," said the voice. "Speaking!"

That set me wondering. Does Durbridge ever frighten himself sitting at his typewriter hammering out frightening dialogue? Does he ever look up from a page and jump at a shadow?

And when the phone rings and he picks up the receiver, does he ever get a chill down his spine as a strange voice asks: "Is Mr Durbridge there?"

Anyway, he sounded relieved when I told him who was calling. (Durbridge writes the Paul Temple strip cartoon published nightly in the *Manchester Evening News*).

My Friend Charles is being cast now. I have high-hopes that William Lucas, whom Durbridge fans remember as the second-hand car dealer will reappear.

"I can understand that," said the author, approvingly. "But contracts have not yet been signed."

The story concerns a Harley Street doctor. More than that Durbridge will not reveal, for fear of spoiling the plot.

But I have his word that it will be in the usual vein. Incidentally, movie people are already inquiring after the film rights, although they have not yet seen the script.

Manchester Evening News

Stephen Murray in Durbridge Serial

Stephen Murray will be seen as Howard Latimer, a Harley Street doctor, in the new Francis Durbridge tv thriller serial. Its title: *My Friend Charles*.

Offices and factories ran sweepstakes on the ending of the last Durbridge serial, but the only safe bet just now is that you won't get the solution to the latest mystery for six weeks.

The author successfully employed his technique of suspense in the Paul Temple sound radio series, and in his tv serials *The Broken Horseshoe, Operation Daybreak* and *The Teckman Biography.*

And finally in *Portrait of Alison* which was made into a film.

Two girls to look for tonight are Gillian Raine, making her tv debut as Latimer's fiancée, and Marianne Brauns as a German film star, in real life Marianne is … a German film star.

Francis Durbridge and producer Alan Bromly (teamed in *Portrait of Alison*) will not comment themselves about the plot beyond saying that Latimer, through no fault of his own, is involved through his connection with his friend Charles Kaufmann, a film producer who though English, has become Americanised by years in the States.

In Episode 1 a telephone call asks Latimer to meet a German film star at London Airport …

Southern Daily Echo

Teleview by **Peter Black**

A new serial by Francis Durbridge, the smoothest arranger of suspense in the business, follows *Tales From Soho* into the Saturday night spot. It stars Stephen Murray who is still not quite certain whether he is playing the hero or the villain.

This comes about through Durbridge's trick of keeping his denouements secret. Only he and his producer, Alan Bromly, know how *My Friend Charles* ends.

Murray plays Howard Latimer, a Harley Street doctor who is involved in mystery through his connection with Charles Kaufmann, a film producer. Kaufmann asks Latimer to meet a German film star arriving at London airport: and that is the beginning of many strange events ...

From the fact that Latimer is described in BBC publicity as "a normal cheerful man in his late 30's and has a fiancée," I deduce that Murray is, after all, the hero. But with Durbridge you can never be certain.

My Friend Charles is Durbridge's first serial since he signed his five-year contract with the BBC last October by which he will provide two tv serials a year. The fee is high, but it is only the beginning, Durbridge serials are turned into films as a matter of course.

Daily Mail

Durbridge Serial On The Way by **David Dewar**

It's a great relief to be able to write about tv programmes in the future tense again without having the uneasy foreboding that before your words appear in print the feature you are writing about will be cancelled.

First and foremost in the things-to-come list is a new serial by Francis Durbridge, who collected record tv thriller fan followings for such serials of yesteryear as *The Broken Horsehsoe, Operation Diplomat, The Teckman Biography* and *Portrait of Alison*.

Durbridge is now on contract to supply two serials a year to BBC television, and the first, *My Friend Charles*, starts on March 10. To obtain information in advance about the plot of a Durbridge serial is about as difficult as to forecast the content of a Soviet Communist Congress. "Keep them in suspense" has always been the Durbridge adage. But I have discovered that the central character is a Dr Latimer, who is rung up one day by a friend, Charles Kaufmann, and asked to meet a German film star at London Airport. He finds (like many Durbridge characters) that a phone call can have momentous complications!

Latimer, who will be played by an actor who has yet to be given the tv Oscar I think he has richly deserved for past performances – Stephen Murray. Marianne Brauns who happens to be a German film star, will take that role in the serial.

Glasgow Evening Times

A new Durbridge Serial for BBC TV on March 10
by **Ken Hankins**
Viewers of BBC television on Saturday nights seem to like nothing better than half-an-hour of suspense and thrills, inserted between those brief and often pointless *In Town Tonight* interviews and a sixty-minute show in the frenzied company of the comedian whose turn to perform has cropped up on the duty roster.

Who better, then, to follow in the dubious footsteps of Mr Mather's odd characters from Soho than Francis Durbridge, the Paul Temple author, who has had some success on tv with previous serials?

The latest on the assembly line is called *My Friend Charles*. It will open on March 10 and concerns a Harley Street doctor, who, in attempting to help out an old chum gets himself involved in what Jimmy Jewel would describe as "a proper carry on."

The accent will be on suspense (an essential ingredient of any serial of this nature) and if Mr Durbridge's four earlier offerings, *The Broken Horseshoe*, *Operation Diplomat, The Teckman Biography* and *Portrait of Alison* are any guide then we stand by for a few surprises long before the final denouement.

Northamptonshire Evening Telegraph

New Francis Durbridge Serial Begins
Stephen Murray, reader of "Who Dunnit" thrillers, is faced with a double mystery in his first serial, tonight's *My Friend Charles*.

As a Harley Street specialist he drives to London Airport to meet a German film star and finds himself involved in a first class riddle. As Stephen Murray his poser is to find if he's hero or villain of the piece.

Veteran tv and radio serialist Francis Durbridge believes in keeping his players as well as his public in suspense and has told nobody, not even producer Alan Bromly, the contents of more than the first three episodes.

Mr Murray is happy about one aspect of the story, however. He plays his own age of 43, one of the few times he has been allowed to do so in the last 20 years. Generally he dodders about as a septuagenarian.

As if one doctor's role was not enough he rolls up at the BBC tomorrow to play a pathologist in a recorded play. There is no mystery about the film star in the serial. She is Marianne Brauns, a German film star in real life.

Northern Despatch

183

New Serial by **Allan Prior**

R.F. Delderfield and Francis Durbridge are two very successful professional authors. One has "made his name" writing thrillers, the other has concentrated on comedies.

Next week on tv, Durbridge plays true to form, but Delderfield is trying something new.

The "D for Durbridge" offering is a new serial (beginning tonight) about a doctor and a detective-inspector, or partly about them, because they both appear in the cast list.

More than that, nobody knows, for *My Friend Charles* is a new serial written specially for tv. Stephen Murray, who doesn't know how to give a poor tv performance, (he's my tip for the next actor's TV Oscar) plays the lead, Dr Latimer.

Charles? There's no "Charles" in the programme list – and as actor-BBC agreements say all actors' names should be shown, there's no "Charles" at all, I suppose.

Worth investigating the mystery? I'd say yes.

Blackpool Gazette and Herald

Last Night's Viewing

Francis Durbridge's serial, *My Friend Charles*, seems a winner. There was murder, mystery, suspense, and, it would seem the supernatural in the first part of this story about a Harley Street doctor.

Sunday Dispatch

Radio & Television

Writers of television thriller serials normally pack plenty of suspense and mystery into the first instalment. Difference with Francis Durbridge is that the viewer can be certain that the excitement will be maintained right up to the final curtain.

Mr Durbridge's latest, *My Friend Charles*, which started on Saturday, has all the ingredients we have come to expect from this prince of story tellers.

How does the brass candlestick seen by the doctor's young patient tie up with the candlestick used to murder the girl found dead in his flat? In his own good time Mr Durbridge will provide an ingenious explanation. We can only watch, wait and thoroughly enjoy ourselves.

Wolverhampton Express & Star

Teleview by **Philip Purser**
Instalment one of Francis Durbridge's new Saturday serial, *My Friend Charles*, was a model of how to ensnare a serial audience.

"Listen, if you like," Mr Durbridge says in effect, "I'll tell you a story."

And starting at the beginning, he began: no tricks, no cheating, no flashbacks. But in half an hour every incident had sprouted a bewildering question mark, leaving a whole thicket of them to puzzle the mind during the coming week.

A Harley Street specialist, Dr Howard Latimer (Stephen Murray) has finished off for the day; his last appointment has been with a mother whose little girl appeared to be suffering from morbid hallucinations – she maintained she had come across the body of a man who had been clubbed to death with a brass candlestick.

As the doctor was about to leave, a man intruded, introducing himself as a journalist. He wished to question Latimer on an article in the *Lancet*.

He wasn't succeeding very well, hardly surprising in view of his unsympathetic approach, when the phone rings. It was the doctor's friend Charles, the Hollywood film producer.

He was on his way to London, but the plane had been diverted to Prestwick. Would Latimer do him a favour and meet a German actress arriving at London Airport?

There was little time to get to Heathrow. The brusque journalist rather surprisingly agreed to drive him in his car.

185

They met the girl and returned to London, the doctor hopping out at Hyde Park Corner to keep an appointment for which he was already late.

Then the question marks began to burgeon; the actress is found murdered – clubbed with a brass candlestick – in the doctor's flat; the journalist is not known on the paper he mentioned; friend Charles never left New York. Things look bad for Dr Latimer – and good for BBC viewing figures.

Daily Mail

Serial's Promise

Nothing has been more eagerly awaited than the Francis Durbridge serial, *My Friend Charles*, and viewers first taste of this new Durbridge dish must have left them wanting more.

We were plunged straight into the affairs of the main character; interest mounted quickly and was maintained throughout; the arrival of the first corpse was contrived with speed and shock.

Mr Durbridge obviously has many more surprises up his sleeve yet, but if he can keep up the standard of episode one he has another sure winner here.

Stephen Murray, playing a pleasant character for a change, is already up to his neck in trouble – though he is in no trouble as far as playing the part is concerned. For the past two years he has been, in my opinion, far and away our best tv actor.

Bradford Telegraph and Argus

Serial Technique Might Be Useful by Irvin Scott

Although I despise the weakness in one that the addiction reveals, I know that I shall be drawn to the television screen at eight o'clock every Saturday evening until the middle of April. The new Francis Durbridge serial, *My Friend Charles*, has me in its grip.

Like almost every other tv serial that ever was it started off by ladling out stiff doses of improbability which, I am sure, hundreds of thousands as well as myself swallowed. One of Francis Durbridge's most important gifts as a writer is the ability to make us believe the well-nigh impossible.

It is closely linked with his handling of suspense. The various points and revelations are made exactly when they will be most effective and most likely to be believed.

The end of the first instalment provided an obvious example of this. The connection between the schoolgirl's supposed hallucination and Dr Latimer's awful fix was revealed just in time to keep us talking and theorising until the next instalment.

The outraged critic in me resists the distortion of real life and the stretching of coincidence which are necessary to this type of mystery thriller, but the other critic in me, who is not so easily scandalised, tells me to relax and enjoy a clever dramatic contrivance. The second critic wins.

Other programmes which set out to win friends and influence people might be helped by having the Durbridge serial technique attached to it. Many television items are at present acceptable enough individually, but lack a compulsive quality to carry them over from week to week.

Crewe Guardian

Everything Stops For Durbridge
That prolific writer Francis Durbridge seems to have come up with another winner in his Saturday night serial, *My Friend Charles*.

Unfortunately, I missed the earlier episode and thus had a little difficulty in getting into the story.

But on Saturday night I was visiting the home of some friends when the weekly dose of Durbridge was screened.

187

These friends are bridge fanatics and the first rubber was at a crucial stage when *My Friend Charles* began.

To my amazement the bridge was suspended by unanimous agreement for 30 minutes. I've never known anything stop their card playing before.

Brighton Evening Argus

Made For The Medium by **G. A. Olden**

Mr Francis Durbridge is one of the few BBC authors who get the Corporation's equivalent of star billing. For instance, his new thriller, *My Friend Charles*, is described in the *Radio Times* as "a Francis Durbridge serial" – a subtle distinction implying that the author's name is of more significance than the nature of his work.

On the whole, *My Friend Charles* is a most welcome addition to Saturday night viewing. Since Nigel Kneale's wildly imaginative *Quatermass II* reached its hare-brained conclusion in outer space, we have been offered a dreary succession of makeshift programmes, *The Adventures of Annabel* were plain stupid, Berkeley Mather's *Tales From Soho* were neatly written but had no consecutive story interest.

Mr Durbridge's yarn (Episode 3 may be seen next Saturday) resembles a Hitchcock screenplay in that its characters appear to have their feet so firmly planted on the ground that one unhesitatingly accepts the decidedly abnormal predicaments they run into. Just as Sherlock Holmes could set our imagination racing with his casual references to the Giant Rat of Sumatra, or the strange affair of Cardinal Tosca, so can Mr Durbridge make us believe that a man's life may depend on the recovery of a book of matches used by a German actress.

Specialists in this *genre* will have noticed a resemblance to Ethel Lina White's *The Wheel Spins* – Durbridge's Dr

188

Latimer has lots of witnesses to establish his innocence, yet the police can patiently prove to him that none of them exists – but the story has quite enough original detail to keep us viewing and guessing. It is also a decidedly "televisual" story, tailor-made for the little screen. Stephen Murray has been playing Dr Latimer almost uncomfortably well, and if the remaining parts sustain the promise of the first two *My Friend Charles* will be remembered as a notable contribution to television drama.

Irish Times

Tantalising Durbridge
How tantalising it is to have to wait a week to find out what's going to happen next in Francis Durbridge's serial thriller, *My Friend Charles*, but what a fascinating, exciting time we're going to spend in getting to the bottom of all the mystery.

We shall be a little dizzy if Mr Durbridge keeps on delivering surprises at the same pace in his third episode, but knowing what a master storyteller he is, no doubt we'll have a pause to recover our breath before he sets us gasping again.

Eastern Evening News

Durbridge Does The Double by Allan Prior
Thriller writer Francis Durbridge does the double this week – tv and radio.

His crime serial *My Friend Charles* moves into Episode Five tonight. And Paul Temple is on sound again Wednesday in the Light Programme.

What makes a dramatic thriller writer this good?

I'd say an ability to surprise.

My Friend Charles isn't a wonderfully well-written piece, and, character-wise, there is almost nothing for the actors to latch on to – hence Stephen Murray's puzzled expression now and again!

But plot wise *My Friend Charles* lifts you out of your seat, hits you between the eyes, grips you, freezes your marrow … well, you get the idea.

Mind, I don't say Mr Durbridge justifies his plots. He simply doesn't bother to. He just drives on to the next surprise.

It works.

So if you like thrillers that aren't crossword puzzles, just plain plot of the kind you can't unravel afterwards, put a cross against Paul Temple and *My Friend Charles*.

Millions will.

Blackpool Gazette and Herald

Durbridge Scores Another Success

One, and possibly two things were quite certain by the time the first instalment of BBC television's new Saturday night serial, *My Friend Charles* had come to an end three weeks ago.

The first was that Francis Durbridge, the author, had another success to his credit. The second: that if they had not already done so, the film moguls will be after Mr Durbridge for the film rights of his latest thriller.

The broadcasting success of Mr Durbridge is a remarkable one. Noted as the writer of the famous sound radio series featuring Paul Temple, he made the transition from sound to vision when the new medium came along just as though there was no difference between the two. And from his pen, effortlessly and regularly, the serials have flowed – *The Broken Horseshoe, The Teckman Biography* and *Portrait of Alison*. Every one was a winner.

And it is nice to note, too, that the man who has been associated with Mr Durbridge in the third and most successful serial, producer Alan Bromly – once a member of the

Northampton Repertory Company – is again in charge of the proceedings.

The Durbridge-Bromly partnership can, indeed, be ranked as one of television's most successful writer-producer combinations and in their newest success they are at it again with instalments endings which every week bring new twists and suggest new situations to the story of the Harley Street doctor and his, so far unseen, friend Charles.

Last Saturday, incidentally, producer Bromly had the pleasure of directing his wife in a small part. June Ellis, a former rep actress, appeared as the shop woman who gave Dr Latimer (Stephen Murray) the parcel which should have contained his fiancee's shoes but instead …?

Northern Independent

Radio and Television Notes by **Pat Hartridge**

As the fascinating Saturday serial, *My Friend Charles,* draws to a close I am beset by an awful feeling that the final episode (to be seen tomorrow night) will be a bit of a let-down. It is easier to build up suspense than to resolve it satisfactorily.

Yet I hope my fears are unfounded because in qualities of construction, acting, dialogue and direction, this six-part thriller by Francis Durbridge must surely be unequalled.

In any event, it will set a hot pace for its successor, *Opportunity Murder*, which starts a week tomorrow, with Anne Crawford and Alexander Knox in the leading roles.

Middlesbrough Evening Gazette

Tonight You'll Know the Villain by **John Moore**

Tonight will come to the end of a tv serial which no doubt kept many viewers in a state of aggravated curiosity with the tortured and mystifying plot.

But I have cheerful news for them.

They haven't been the only ones who have been puzzled by *My Friend Charles*.

So have the cast.

Particularly actor Stephen Murray – who has been making a first-class job of the leading role, as Dr Howard Latimer.

Throughout the five episodes so far Dr Latimer has worn a look of almost dazed bewilderment – befitting a man who has been surrounded by sinister characters with an unending supply of aliases. Men and women who aren't the people he or the viewers have thought they were. Specialists in double-talk and riddles.

The funny thing is that he really has been bewildered.

Stephen Murray – rehearsing for the sixth and final instalment tonight – told a London colleague of mine that until he and the rest of the cast were handed their scripts on Monday none of them had an inkling of the villain's identity.

"It came as a great surprise to all of us," he said – and added, "But I can't give you even a hint without spoiling the whole thing."

Stephen Murray won't even tell his 11-year-old daughter Amanda, who can't see tonight's last episode because she is taking part in a swimming gala.

My Friend Charles has been a great success and not only because of this Chinese-puzzle of a plot.

The pace has never slackened and the sets and setting have never appeared skimped in any way.

Finishing a serial like this is usually one of the most difficult problems to face the producer. For the sake of what has gone before I hope Episode 6 is a real success tonight.

Even Parties Stop For The Serial! By **Lucille Iremonger**
On Saturday night I went to a party. It had been going for an hour when I arrived, and I knew there were a couple of dozen

people inside the house. Several cars were parked outside, and lights streamed out into the drive.

Yet not a sound reached us as we stood outside the front door.

Loud shushes greeted us as we made our way in.

Quite half the party stood rapt and silent in the front room – before the tv set (the other half had taken refuge in the back room).

They were listening to the last instalment of Francis Durbridge's serial *My Friend Charles*. A tactful host had decided that no guest of his should suffer any deprivation by coming to his party.

Everyone was happy, both those who liked looking in and those it drove mad.

But what would have been the arrangement if the host had possessed only one communal room? Who would have had to give way?

Ilford Recorder

Contrast In New Detection Serial
Now that Francis Durbridge has relieved actor Stephen Murray of the expression of bewilderment he wore throughout that excellent thriller serial *My Friend Charles* (in his role as Dr Howard Latimer), we look back on its six episodes with considerable pleasure.

Mr Durbridge is without equal as a creator of the smoothly mechanical plot, brimming over with surprises, seemingly impossible to untangle within the space of half an hour, yet so simply solved in the end. He compels, he fascinates, he tantalises – but even when all his secrets are laid bare, we are still a little mystified.

We have seen the jigsaw picture finished before our very eyes, but so many pieces have fallen into place, we have been so dazzled by the author's legerdemain, that when it's all over and we stop to think about it, we realise we'd never win a prize for explaining exactly why so many puzzling, exciting things happened to Dr Latimer.

It was splendid while it lasted, and logical enough when we watched the disentanglement in Part 6 – and that's all that really matters.

Eastern Evening News